MANDY MORTON began her professional life as a musician. More recently, she has worked as a freelance arts journalist for national and local radio. She currently presents the radio arts magazine *The Eclectic Light Show* and lives with her partner, who is also a crime writer, in Cambridge and Cornwall, where there is always a place for an ageing long-haired tabby cat.

@icloudmandy
@hettiebagshot
HettieBagshotMysteries

*The Ghost of Christmas Paws*

MANDY MORTON

Allison & Busby Limited
12 Fitzroy Mews
London W1T 6DW
*allisonandbusby.com*

First published in Great Britain by Allison & Busby in 2016.

A CIP catalogue record for this book is available from
the British Library.

First Edition

ISBN 978-0-7490-1906-8

Typeset in 11.5/16.6 pt Sabon by
Allison & Busby Ltd.

The paper used for this Allison & Busby publication
has been produced from trees that have been legally sourced
from well-managed and credibly certified forests.

Printed and bound by
CPI Group (UK) Ltd, Croydon, CR0 4YY

*For Nicola, and in memory of*
*Sooty Perkins – an excellent Cornish cat*

# CHAPTER ONE

The early arrival of winter was taking its toll on the town. Since the middle of November, the residents had been cloaked in icy fog and torrential rain, punctuated by two heavy falls of snow, which – though beautiful – had driven cats indoors and brought life to a standstill. Now, with only a week to go before Christmas, a new threat had come knocking: a virulent strain of cat flu, which was sweeping the town with terrible consequences.

Local businesses had closed their doors in a vain attempt to stop the flu spreading. Elsie Haddock hadn't fried so much as a chip for two weeks in her popular high-street fish emporium; Hilda Dabit had abandoned her dry-cleaning business and taken to her bed; and even Shroud and Trestle, undertakers, were running a skeleton staff. Malkin and Sprinkle, the town's department store, had been forced to impose the wearing of face masks in their food hall to fight the germs, and the haberdashery department had been closed altogether since Lotus Ping collapsed behind her counter in a bout of violent sneezing, upending the button cupboard and burying herself in an avalanche of fancy fastenings. Turner Page's newly opened library had closed its doors for fear of the flu being spread via the books, and he had offered his mobile library van as an overnight shelter with hot soup and biscuits for cats who had no permanent refuge from the weather.

There had been a number of fatalities, although it was hard to say how many as most sufferers had isolated themselves and were dying unnoticed in their beds. Agnes Featherstone Clump, the local district nurse, was at her wits' end in trying to administer to the population, and if Irene Peggledrip, the town's psychic, hadn't offered her house as a makeshift field hospital, more cats would have been awaiting burial in Shroud and Trestle's refrigeration unit.

Betty and Beryl Butter's pie and pastry shop was one of the few businesses still standing, and served as a beacon of hope in a sea of coughing and spluttering. Beryl herself had succumbed in the early days of the outbreak but her sister carried on bravely, keeping the bread ovens fired up and administering large mugs of beef tea to her flu-ridden sibling, nursing her back to health in time to dress the Christmas window.

The No. 2 Feline Detective Agency had its offices in the old storeroom behind the Butters' shop, and was run by Hettie Bagshot and her sidekick Tilly Jenkins. The two tabbies had earned themselves quite a reputation in recent months, having solved several high-profile murder cases and a number of minor thefts involving a Battenberg cake and a large wedge of French Brie. Like most offices in the town, the Detective Agency was closed and had been transformed into a cosy bedsitter for the two cats to lie low in until the ravages of the epidemic died down. Their rent included luncheon vouchers to be exchanged in the Butters' shop and as much coal as their fireplace could consume, and had it not been for Lavender Stamp, postmistress, who sneezed all over Tilly as she delivered her Christmas catalogues, all would have been well.

Tilly was having a terrible night of coughing and sneezing, falling in and out of a delirious state that began to frighten Hettie as she paced the floor, doubtful of her friend's ability to withstand the killer virus. She watched as Tilly tossed and turned on her cushion in front of the fire, first hot and bathed in sweat as her fur clung to her, then shivering with cold, her breath slow and rasping. This was Hettie's third night of vigil, and a brief visit from Agnes Featherstone Clump only confirmed what she knew in her heart: Tilly was in grave danger, and the next few days would be crucial.

Her friendship with Tilly had surprised her. Hettie wasn't the sort of cat to form lasting relationships of any kind, and her life had been a chequered journey of stormy seas, energetic endeavours and a host of brilliant ideas that never quite saw the light of day. With Tilly it was different: encouraged by her simple view of life – a good dinner, an open fire and a warm blanket at the end of each day – Hettie had never been happier, but there was a strong chance now that her own warm blanket was about to be pulled from under her.

She shivered, only partly from the cold, and pulled her dressing gown closer, eyeing the small pile of Christmas presents neatly stacked in the corner by the staff sideboard – the last thing that Tilly had done before falling ill. She had spent two days battling with sticky tape and labels under a makeshift tent so that Hettie's prying eyes wouldn't spoil the surprises procured from Jessie's charity shop, and she had been so excited – even more so when Hettie suggested that their coffers could run to a real Christmas tree to show the parcels off to their best advantage. That was several days ago now, and the prospect of Christmas had held very little magic in Hettie's mind since; the very thought of facing it without her friend was unbearable.

Hettie tiptoed across to the fire to add some more coal, careful not to wake Tilly now that she had finally fallen into a deep sleep. Their friend Bruiser, who lived in a shed at the bottom of the Butters' garden, had brought in some apple logs as a get-well present and Hettie selected one and placed it in the middle of the coals. Everyone was so kind, and Tilly was getting the best possible care, but would it be enough? She was older than Hettie, riddled with arthritis, and had lost several teeth during years of living rough before an invitation to share Hettie's small rented room had changed her life.

There was a gentle tap on the door and Hettie responded immediately, hoping that Tilly would sleep on. The imposing form of Betty Butter stood in the hallway, proffering two steaming mugs of beef tea and a selection of savoury tarts, fresh from the oven. 'And how is the patient today?' she whispered, handing over the tray.

'Not good. She's had an awful night and I'm so worried about her. I don't know what to do for the best.'

Betty glanced at the heap of blankets by the fire, watching the rise and fall of Tilly's laboured breathing. 'Don't you give up. Our old mother always used to say that there's nowt to shout about till the undertakers are coming down the path.'

Hettie knew that the handed-down pearls of Lancashire wisdom were meant well, but she found no real comfort in Betty's words. Her tired eyes lingered on the savouries, hoping that they might give her the strength to fight some of the darker thoughts that had engulfed her during the night. 'Thank you for the tea and pastries,' she said. 'They look lovely. I'll see if I can get Tilly to drink something when she wakes up.'

Betty bustled back to the shop and Hettie shut the door quietly behind her. She collapsed into the armchair by the fire, suddenly too tired to eat or drink, leaving the beef tea and tarts untouched on the table.

# CHAPTER TWO

How long the two cats slept was hard to say, but it was Tilly who woke first, pleased to find that she felt much better. Abandoning her blankets, she stared out of the window in sheer delight: a thick covering of snow had fallen in the Butters' backyard overnight, and a pale winter sun made everything bright and sparkling. 'Ooh lovely!' she cried, clapping her arthritic paws together. 'I hope it stays till Christmas. I *love* Christmas!'

Tilly's joy was rudely interrupted by the appearance of Lavender Stamp in the yard, laden down with her postbag. She pulled her cardigan on over her pyjamas and met the postmistress at the back door, relieving her of a sack full of Christmas cards for the Butters and a single letter addressed to the No. 2 Feline Detective Agency, postmarked Cornwall. Returning to their room, she turned the letter over in her paws and noticed that it had been sealed with bright red wax and stamped with what appeared to be a baronial crest.

Hettie – feeling the icy blast from the open door – was slowly coming to her senses after a good long sleep, and smiled with relief to see Tilly up and about. 'Who was that at the door?' she asked, struggling into her dressing gown.

'Lavender Stamp. And look – we've got a very important letter.'

Hettie did her best to focus on the object of Tilly's enthusiasm as it was waved in front of her. 'Why is it important?' she demanded, snatching the letter from Tilly's paws. 'We're not expecting anything important.'

Tilly watched as Hettie examined the letter, willing her to open it. Her friend looked closely at the seal, then sniffed the envelope. 'I thought so,' she said, sniffing it again. 'Fish. That's what it is – fish. And look at the seal – it's a crab on some sort of coat of arms.' Tilly sniffed the envelope at Hettie's invitation and had to agree that the letter did indeed have a very strong smell of fish. 'I suppose we'd better open it,' Hettie said thoughtfully. 'Although I'm not very happy about getting letters from cats we don't know. It's a bit of a bloody cheek if you ask me.'

Tilly ignored Hettie's comment, fearing that it would turn into a full-blown rant about the invasion of her personal space. Instead, she put the kettle on and loaded the toaster with two slices of bread, knowing that they would both be in a much better state of mind after they'd eaten. The letter sat unopened on the mantelpiece while they chewed and licked their way through two rounds of toast, thickly spread with cheese triangles and washed down with two mugs of hot tea. Finally, after much cleaning of ears, paws and whiskers, Hettie reached for the envelope.

'Now then, let's see what this is all about,' she said, breaking the seal with her sharpest claw.

'Oh do read it out loud so we both know together,' cried Tilly, climbing onto the arm of Hettie's chair so that she could look over her shoulder.

The letter appeared to have been through several wars. It was splashed with mud and gave off a much stronger smell of fish than had been hinted at by its envelope. Noting the same coat of arms on the letterhead, Hettie began to read, allowing herself to lapse into a mild Cornish accent for greater effect.

*Lady Eloise Crabstock-Singe*
*Crabstock Manor*
*Porthladle*
*Cornwall*

*Dear Miss Bagshot,*
*I understand that you take on the solvin' of murders and the like, and I would be most obliged if you could sort out a crime that 'as 'aunted my family for years – and it's still 'appenin'!*

15

*It is most urgent and I fear for my life. As I am the only one left, I'm next! I know it's comin' up to Christmas, but that's when it 'appens if it's goin' to 'appen, and she 'as been seen twice in the kitchen and once on the stairs since December arrived.*

*I am enclosin' two train tickets for Bodkin Moor Station, as you should not come on your own. I shall 'ave you collected and taken to Jam Makers Inn overnight, then on to Crabstock Manor the next day. I shall expect you on 20th December, and shall order your rooms to be made ready dreckly.*

*I will pay you in more gold than you can ever spend if you save my life.*

*In 'opes,*

*Eloise Crabstock-Singe*

*Lady of Crabstock Manor, Porthladle, and all surroundin' fields and allotments.*


'Well, that's completely ridiculous!' said Hettie, tossing the letter aside. 'Sounds like something from one of those penny dreadfuls you bring home from Turner Page's library. It must be a hoax of some sort.'

Ignoring the slight on her reading habits, Tilly tipped the envelope upside down and two train tickets floated down onto the hearth rug. 'The tickets are real enough. They're dated for tomorrow, the 19th, and Christmas in Cornwall in a big old mansion

16

sounds so exciting! We can have our own Christmas when we get back.' She began to dance round the room, finding it hard to contain herself as Hettie read the letter again.

'Well, I'm not saying we can't go,' Hettie said at last. 'But this could all be a wild goose chase.'

'A wild seagull!' corrected Tilly. 'They have seagulls in Cornwall.'

Hettie ignored the interruption and pushed on with her concerns. 'You haven't been well, and it's a very long way to Cornwall. The weather's bad and there are bound to be cancellations and hold-ups. Do we really want to get stuck in a snowdrift on Bodkin Moor?' Tilly's heart leapt at such an exciting prospect, and she gave very little thought to the harsh reality of Hettie's words. 'And then there's the crime itself – who is 'SHE' who hangs round in the kitchen and on the stairs, and why is this Eloise Crabstock-Twinge the last one standing? This letter gives us very little to go on, and don't they have aitches in Cornwall?'

Tilly giggled as she struggled to pull a battered old suitcase out from under the staff sideboard, bringing a multitude of cobwebs, dust balls and stray custard creams with it. 'If we're going to take the job, you'd better start calling her Singe and not Twinge. These aristocats lay great store by their names. And Cornwall may not have aitches, but it is the official home of PASTIES!'

Hettie gave up trying to be sensible and joined Tilly in

her endeavours to pack everything they would need for the long journey ahead: hats, mittens and scarves; three of Tilly's best cardigans and two pairs of Hettie's warm business slacks with matching striped polo neck jumpers; winceyette pyjamas; long woolly socks; Tilly's penguin hot-water bottle that Hettie had bought for her the Christmas before; and Hettie's catnip pouch and pipe.

After a struggle and much swearing, the lid to the overburdened suitcase was finally closed and the safety catches snapped into place. 'I think you'll have to take your tartan shopper as well,' suggested Hettie. 'We'll need to take food and drink for the train, and God knows what home comforts will be on offer at Jam Makers Inn! I'll ask Bruiser to run us to the station in Scarlet. It'll be a bit of a squeeze but we'll manage somehow.'

Miss Scarlet was the No. 2 Feline Detective Agency's official mode of transport, a shiny red motorbike and sidecar christened by Tilly after a character in her favourite board game and skilfully driven by Bruiser, an old friend of Hettie's who had become indispensable to the agency and to the Butter sisters as their 'lad about the yard' – so indispensable, in fact, that the Butters had provided a purpose-built shed for Bruiser and Miss Scarlet to live in at the bottom of their vegetable patch.

Hettie pulled on some warm clothes and – after locating her wellingtons, which she eventually found in the second drawer of their filing cabinet – trudged down the snowy garden path to inform Bruiser of their travel plans. Tilly rescued her tartan shopper from its parking space by one of the bread ovens and sat at the table making a list of the foods they would need for the journey. By the time she'd finished, she'd filled two sides of a piece of paper and was beginning to wonder whether the restaurant car on the train might be a better idea. Remembering what Hettie had said about the possibility of delays and cancellations, she eventually decided to stick with her list, trimming it down a little before leaving it on the table for Hettie's final approval. Then she dressed herself in one of her 'at home' cardigans and set about tidying their room and dragging the suitcase out into the back hallway for their early morning departure.

It was some time before Hettie returned. Tilly watched from the window until she came into view as a dark shape in the middle of a rather thick snow flurry. She skipped to the back door, ready to assist with the wellingtons which always seemed to fit on very easily and refuse to come off without collective acts of extreme violence. To make matters worse, the wellingtons were caked in frozen snow. Hettie sat on the door mat while Tilly pulled with all her strength until eventually boot one gave way with such force that she shot across the hallway, landing in an ungainly heap by one of the bread ovens, the wellington still firmly between her paws. The second boot surrendered with much less effort and the two cats stumbled back into their room to warm their icy paws by the fire.

'Bruiser said he's been to Porthladle,' said Hettie, getting a crumpled map out of the staff sideboard. 'He says it's full of sardines and old cats mending fishing nets.'

'Well, we like sardines so that's a good thing,' said Tilly, trying to remain positive and hoping that Hettie wasn't about to change her mind about their trip.

'Look – here's Porthladle, and Crabstock Manor's marked. It looks like it's hanging off a cliff! Bruiser says the coast round there has the worst storms in the whole of Cornwall, and as for Jam Makers Inn, he reckons there's something odd about the place but he can't quite remember what it is.' Hettie struggled with the map until she had located Bodkin Moor. 'Well, I doubt that many travellers stop off there. It's in the middle of nowhere and not even marked on the map as far as I can see.'

Tilly scanned the area that Hettie had pointed to and finally settled on a spot marked with a cross. 'That'll be it. They always put inns at crossroads in films, and that's where the two paths that cross the moor meet.'

'You wouldn't want to be stuck out there without a pie and a packet of crisps on a cold night, would you?' muttered Hettie, as she folded the map and put it ready to take with them.

'Speaking of pies,' said Tilly, reaching for her list, 'what do you think to this? I've allowed for elevenses, lunch, afternoon tea, dinner and supper, with a few extras for emergencies just in case Jam Makers Inn doesn't do food.'

Hettie looked down the list, impressed enough to read it out loud, much to Tilly's delight, and she listened as if hearing it for the first time. 'Ham rolls, flapjack, egg and bacon tarts, fresh cream scones, cheese scones, iced fancies, beef and ale pie, salmon turnovers, crisps (2 x plain, 2 x Marmite), sausage rolls, cream horns and two bottles of fiery ginger beer. I see you've crossed out the cheese baps and Betty's iced Christmas novelty biscuits – I think they should stay if you can fit them in. It's a very long way to Cornwall, and you need building up.'

Tilly was thrilled with Hettie's approval and wasted no time in pulling on her own wellingtons to trudge round to the front of the Butters' shop to place her order. The rest of the day was spent in writing Christmas cards and sending notes to friends, informing them of their imminent departure. Tilly had exchanged their luncheon vouchers for a steak and kidney pie, and the two cats dined early, watching the evening news and an episode of *Top Cat* before turning in for an early night, hoping to wake refreshed for whatever the next few days would bring.

# CHAPTER THREE

Bruiser was ready and waiting in the high street as Hettie and Tilly struggled with their luggage, slipping and sliding on snow that had become slushy and difficult to negotiate. Tilly's tartan shopper had stalled with iced-up wheels, and Bruiser applied all his strength to hauling it into Scarlet's sidecar along with the battered suitcase and Tilly herself. Hettie – who rarely rode pillion – climbed up behind Bruiser as a matter of necessity, and the three cats sped off to the town's railway station, waved off by Betty and Beryl.

The Bodkin Moor Express stood silently on its rails as Hettie and Tilly approached platform two in hopeful expectation of departing promptly – but an abrupt and rather aggressive announcement from the tannoy system was just the start of a day splattered

22

with difficulties. 'The train now standing at platform two is the three minutes past seven service to Bodkin Moor, stopping at Much-Purring-on-the-Rug, Much-Purring-on-the-Mat, Southwool Junction, Biscuit Garden City, Crunch-on-the-Marsh, Bristle, Lost Whistle, Clotted Cream Parkway, Dark Moor Junction, Piddle-on-the-Cushion, Clawberry Fields, Pasty Tor, and Bodkin Moor. All passengers wishing to continue into Cornwall will have to get off there and make their own arrangements, on account of there being the wrong sort of snow. We would like to point out that this train is running late and, at the moment, it isn't running at all because the driver has got himself snowed in and is digging his way out of Sheba Gardens as I speak – so you'll all just have to wait as he's got the key to the train.'

'Bloody marvellous!' said Hettie, pulling her collar up against the bitter icy wind blowing down the platform. 'It's going to be the best Christmas ever. I can't wait for the cat flu and frostbite to set in.'

Tilly giggled. 'At least we won't starve. Betty and Beryl added some extras to our list. Would a sausage roll and a hot cup of tea help? They packed a flask for us, and it's in the top of my shopper so I could put my paws on it easily. I've got the sausage rolls in my cardigan pockets, just in case we needed them quickly.'

Hettie marvelled at the way in which Tilly could turn a difficult situation into a positive treat, and stamped

23

her feet patiently as the vacuum flask dispensed two hot, sweet, steaming cups of tea. The tea was just what was needed, and the sausage rolls – still warm from Tilly's cardigan pockets – were a small bit of pastry heaven. The vacuum flask had been stowed away in the tartan shopper and the pastry crumbs picked clean from Hettie and Tilly's greatcoats before the driver of the Bodkin Moor Express hoved into view, flustered and apologetic as he turned the key on the dormant train, bringing it instantly to life and allowing the passengers to settle themselves in their seats at last.

Tilly could hardly contain her excitement and found them a compartment close to the refreshment car, just in case they needed a top-up of supplies. Hettie struggled to fit the suitcase into the luggage rack above her head and decided to leave the tartan shopper where they could get at it. She didn't need the tannoy system to remind her of how long the journey was, and the sausage roll would be a distant memory by the time they reached the first stop on their journey.

The Bodkin Express moved slowly out of the town's station. No sooner had it begun to pick up speed than the brakes were applied, just in time to come to a shuddering halt alongside platform one at Much-Purring-on-the-Rug. Hettie sighed. 'Why they need a station at Much-Purring I'll never know. Bloody farm cats and posh folk pretending to live in the country at weekends, stomping about in their waxed jackets.' Hettie brought her thoughts on rural life to an abrupt conclusion as their compartment was invaded by an unruly collection of kittens, bouncing excitedly off the seats while their mother – oblivious to anything except her *Cat's Own* magazine – settled herself opposite Hettie and immersed herself in the latest celebrity gossip.

If it hadn't been for Tilly's swift action, the tartan shopper might well have spilt its contents all over the carriage floor when a rather thuggish looking kitten decided to use it as a springboard into the luggage rack. To make matters worse, if that was possible, the prettiest of the kittens launched into a rather off-key rendition of 'Good King Wenceslas', which started as a small, solitary wail before gathering pace to reach a horrific cacophony of sound as her siblings joined in one by one.

Hettie eyed up the communication cord, wondering if the shattering of her peace and quiet was reason enough to avoid the fine promised by the unnecessary halting of the train, but the train slowed and stopped before she could decide, allowing the mother, her magazine and her army of hooligans to alight at Much-Purring-on-the-Mat. When peace had been restored, she leapt up and rifled the tartan shopper's pouch pocket for notepad and pen, and scribbled a notice which she fixed to the outside of the compartment, sliding the door shut with great satisfaction and slumping back in her seat. Several cats looking for seats stopped in the corridor, read the note and passed on down the train, leaving Hettie and Tilly to enjoy their privacy.

'What did you write?' asked Tilly, spreading herself out across the seat opposite Hettie and opening her copy of *Cat of the Baskervilles*.

'"Cat flu! Enter at your own risk",' said Hettie, picking up her *Daily Snout* and setting about the crossword.

# CHAPTER FOUR

The morning passed without further interruption. By one o'clock, Tilly had become deeply involved in the puzzling case that Holmes and Watson had taken on, and Hettie – having stalled at seven across – had turned her attention to the view from the window, watching the counties slip by cloaked in their snowy landscape.

Beryl's flapjacks were polished off during a longer than planned stop at Crunch-on-the-Marsh, where a grossly overweight elderly cat had somehow become wedged between a luggage trolley and a large stack of fresh fish boxes. Hettie and Tilly watched from their carriage window, gleefully nibbling on their biscuits as the cat in question had to be surgically removed by a forklift truck and deposited in the station buffet while a legion of station personnel scampered about the

27

platform collecting scattered fish. 'Lunchtime!' said Hettie, folding up her virtually unsolved crossword and eyeing up the tartan shopper.

Tilly responded immediately, as if she'd been looking for an excuse to abandon Holmes and Watson, who were suddenly far less exciting than the prospect of the Butters' pastry. 'How about one or two egg and bacon tarts, followed by an iced fancy?' she suggested, locating a greaseproof paper parcel on which Betty had written 'E. and B. T.s'.

'Sounds good. Even better with a shared bag of crisps.' Hettie moved over to Tilly's side of the carriage and laid out two festive paper napkins from a pack that Beryl had included in the shopper. 'I wonder who'll meet us off the train? Jam Makers Inn seems to be some way from the station, and this weather is getting worse as we move west. I can't believe we're doing this.'

Tilly had to agree as she glanced out of the window and realised that she could see nothing but a swirling blizzard which threatened to engulf the train. 'It is getting a bit nasty out there,' she said, wedging a whole savoury tart into her mouth. 'And we haven't even got to the moors yet. It's just like that Agatha Crispy novel where the train gets stuck in the snow.'

'But we're not stuck in the snow,' said Hettie, tugging the crisps open. On cue, the Bodkin Express lurched to an ungainly halt, sending the iced fancies flying across the carriage and scattering the crisps like confetti over the seats. 'Well, that's all we need.' She rescued the iced fancies as Tilly did her best to scoop up the crisps. 'What was the name of that last station we stopped at?'

'I think it was Clotted Cream Parkway, which means that the next one must be Dark Moor Junction.' Tilly consulted a timetable which someone had obligingly stuffed down the side of her seat. 'We still have quite a long way to go and I can't see a platform out of the window, so my guess is we're stuck between stations.'

'Is that a polite way of saying we're in the middle of bloody nowhere?' Hettie asked wearily. 'I'd better go and see what's happening.' She slid the compartment door open, letting in a howling draught, and disappeared into the corridor. Tilly tidied away their half-finished lunch and waited for news.

It was some time before Hettie returned. Her wellingtons were covered in snow and her whiskers – which could never be described as tidy – sported droplets of ice; the look on her face told Tilly that all was not well, and she braced herself for bad news.

Pulling her greatcoat down from the luggage rack, Hettie draped it round her shoulders and began her sorry tale. 'It would appear that the Bodkin Express has been the victim of an avalanche – or, to be more accurate, a giant snowball has tumbled down the hillside onto the track. In the words of the ticket inspector, who I assume by his accent is Cornish, "we'll 'ave ta dig 'er out dreckly, on account of the weather getting worse." I can't help but think that sort of observation errs on the side of the obvious.'

Tilly giggled at her friend's impersonation of a Cornish accent, in spite of the difficult situation they found themselves in. 'Do you think we should go and help?'

'Absolutely no point,' Hettie replied, retrieving an abandoned iced fancy from the shopper. 'I got out to have a look, and there's about six of them taking it in turns with one spade and a saucepan from the buffet car. The snow is so deep out there that it would come up over your head. No, the best place for us is in our carriage, wrapped in our coats. We'll just have to sit it out.'

It was another hour before the giant snowball was cleared from the track. Hettie and Tilly had burrowed into their greatcoats and fallen asleep, and it was the sudden lurch of the train that woke them. Disorientated at first, Hettie sat up with a start and took a moment or two to get her bearings. The blizzard had stopped and the landscape from the window was beautiful. Tilly yawned and stretched and stared at the wonderland before them. 'Oooh! Isn't it lovely? I've never seen so much snow, and look at the twinkly lights coming on in those houses.'

Hettie had to agree that the view from the train was spectacular, but she was becoming more and more concerned. 'It's starting to get dark. We must be running at least two hours late and we've no idea how long it's going to take to get to Bodkin Moor. What if the cat from Jam Makers Inn can't get to us? We'll be stranded.'

Tilly shivered at the prospect, no longer as enthusiastic for a snowy adventure and wishing with all her heart that they were back in their cosy room in front of a roaring fire. The train slowed into Dark Moor Junction and barely gave the passengers time to get on or off before it gathered speed again, heading for Piddle-on-the-Cushion. Hettie decided that they needed a hot drink to cheer their spirits. 'Time for afternoon tea, I think. See if you can locate something cakey from your shopper and I'll try my luck in the buffet car. We need warming up before we're faced with the delights of Bodkin Moor.' Tilly instantly perked up and set about the greaseproof parcels as Hettie made her way next door to the restaurant carriage.

The purchase of two hot chocolates was never going to be a simple matter. Hettie had already accepted that, but what awaited her was beyond her wildest nightmares. The railway employee who ran the hot drinks and snacks kiosk wasn't running anything at all; short-haired and tiger-striped, and resplendent in an equally striped uniform-issue waistcoat, he sat behind

31

his counter with all his paws bandaged, weeping in an uncontrollable manner. Another member of staff, dressed in a rather grubby boiler suit, was doing his best to serve a straggling line of frozen passengers, who – like Hettie – were hopeful of a hot drink. Between sobs, the injured cat – Thomas, according to his name badge – was trying to instruct his deputy in the mysteries of the espresso machine, but "Arry was 'aving trouble 'olding the mug straight' as the frother did its job and spraying the cats at the front of the queue with scalding hot milk. The silver lining from Hettie's point of view was that the scalded cats retreated to fill in accident report forms, leaving her next in line. She ordered two hot chocolates and stood back at a safe distance while the frother did its worst.

'Arry triumphantly slammed the two mugs down on the counter, confident enough now to pass the time of day. "E's got the frostbite, yer see. 'E 'ad ta use 'is pan in the snow. We're 'oping 'is claws don't fall out. I'm on engines usually, see.'

Hettie did see very clearly and selected the perfect sympathetic face as she counted out the right money and retreated to the sanity of her compartment, where Tilly had laid out an afternoon tea fit to cheer any difficult journey. 'I've chosen ham rolls and fresh cream scones,' she said. 'I've saved the big stuff till later in case we really do get stuck.'

Hettie approved of Tilly's choice and entertained

her with a re-enactment of the Thomas and 'Arry show as they made their way through the teatime spread. The hot chocolate was surprisingly good and, by the time the train finally pulled into Bodkin Moor Station, their spirits were high and they were ready to face whatever was to come. Which was just as well, under the circumstances.

# CHAPTER FIVE

The platform at Bodkin Moor Station was deserted. It was the end of the line, and Hettie and Tilly were the only passengers to alight from the train, together with the driver and a handful of bedraggled railway staff. They shuffled past as Hettie struggled with the suitcase, leaving Tilly to slip and slide with the tartan shopper. It was dark now, and only the snow which had blown in onto the platform lit their way as they headed for the exit. They passed the ticket office, where a large grey cat sat reading his paper, oblivious to any arrivals or departures. Hettie hesitated, wondering whether to ask him if there had been anyone waiting to meet them, but he turned away to stoke a cheery fire, avoiding any possibility of conversation and treating her as completely invisible.

'Let's get out of here,' she said, dragging the suitcase across the snow. 'There's bound to be a taxi or a bus out front even if there's no one to meet us. The train staff must have some sort of transport to get them home.'

Hettie was wrong. The railway staff had melted away without a trace and the area normally used as a car park was several feet deep in drifted snow. The landscape was eerie and silent as they emerged from the station, and there was no hint of a footprint in the freshly fallen snow. In front of them was the vast expanse of Bodkin Moor – nothing for miles but the occasional rise of a hill, or, in the near distance, trees which stood like giant snow warriors, their branches contorted by the extreme weather for which the moor was so famous.

Tilly's face said it all. 'I'm so sorry I brought us here. I thought it would be an adventure, but you were right – it is a wild goose chase. Now we're miles away from home, cold and with nowhere to go and, to make matters worse, I've probably ruined Christmas.'

Tilly's sobs fractured the snowy silence as Hettie moved to comfort her, but a noise from behind them stopped her in her tracks – a grunt, followed by something slightly more intelligible. 'You'll be needin' the waiting room, my 'ansomes. Nothing getting through tonight.'

Hettie turned to see the grey station cat, now

35

cloaked against the cold and swinging an oil lantern as he beckoned them back into the station. They followed as he strode down the platform, and watched as he removed a large ring of keys from under his cloak and unlocked the door to a small room which had probably never seen better days. The decor was railway brown, there was a hard, no-nonsense bench pushed against the wall, and an aspidistra in a giant pot which crouched by a set of filthy windows in vain hope of some daylight. The only glimmer of comfort was a small fireplace blackened with age, its tile surround cracked and broken. The grate was empty, and the fall of soot suggested that it had been for some time.

The grey cat shuffled out of the waiting room without another word, leaving Hettie and Tilly to get used to their new surroundings. Tilly parked her tartan shopper in the corner of the room, which made things look instantly more cheerful. 'At least we're out of the snow and we've plenty of food to keep us going,' she said, desperately trying to regain a positive outlook on their situation.

Hettie glanced at the empty grate and shivered. 'We won't last the night in these temperatures. I wonder if Bodkin Moor Station could run to a shovel of coal?'

As if by magic the waiting-room door was flung open and the grey cat stumbled across the floor with a coal scuttle and a bundle of sticks. 'I'll 'ave to get back to me office in case I'm needed, but you can get yerselves a blaze going if you've a mind to.' Their makeshift host set down the scuttle, pulled a box of matches out of his pocket, handed them to Hettie with a grunt, and left them to it.

Hettie wasted no time in laying the fire, and Tilly added some greaseproof paper from the shopper to give the sticks a better chance of lighting. The coals crackled in the grate as the flames took hold, burning blue with the frost from the chimney. There was very little heat to start with, so Hettie dragged the bench in front of the fireplace and they sat together to warm their paws, their greatcoats pulled close around them to stave off the icy draught at their backs.

'We'll have to make a plan,' Hettie said, finally gaining control of teeth that had been chattering away to themselves. 'I think we should write this one off as a bad job and get the first train home in the morning. It's cost us nothing, and we've still got a few days to put on a proper Christmas.'

Tilly had kicked off her wellingtons, and she wriggled her feet with joy as the heat of the fire warmed them through. 'That would be lovely. Betty and Beryl have invited us up to their flat for Christmas dinner, so we should have a wonderful time.'

Hettie was pleased that Tilly was feeling better. There had been too many sad days in her friend's early life, and she had made it her business to ensure that Tilly was safe and happy. 'It's time for one of Betty's best pies, I think,' she said, getting to her feet and wheeling the shopper over to the fire.

There were plenty of greaseproof parcels left and together they carefully unpacked them until they located the package labelled 'B. and A. P.'. 'Here they are,' said Tilly. 'Shall we have a bottle of fiery ginger beer with them?'

'Perfect. I think we'll go for another packet of crisps as well – let's have the Marmite ones this time.'

The Butters' beef and ale pies had never tasted so good and the fiery ginger beer completed the thaw by warming the two cats from the inside. The fire was now roaring up the chimney as if it, too, had been saved from the cold, and when the meal was over they settled down to doze and wait for the morning and the first train back to civilisation.

# CHAPTER SIX

There are many types of civilisation, depending on what you're used to. Less than an hour later, Hettie and Tilly's warm cocoon was shattered by the arrival of Absalom Tweek, landlord of Jam Makers Inn. 'You're fetched!' he shouted, flinging open the waiting-room door.

Startled, Hettie nearly slipped from the bench and Tilly hid behind her, afraid that they were about to be murdered. Hettie stared at the tall, gangly cat, cloaked from head to foot against the weather, and wearing a wide-brimmed hat pulled down low over his craggy face. One steely blue eye surveyed the room like a Cyclops; the other was obscured by a patch and played no part in the inspection.

Hettie stood up, leaving Tilly to gather herself, and their visitor spoke again. 'You're fetched to Jam Makers

Inn. The 'orse'll freeze if we don't get on.' Leaving Hettie to translate what had just been said, the cat picked up their suitcase and strode out into the night.

With no opportunity for discussion, Hettie grabbed Tilly – who was trying to put her wellingtons back on – and the tartan shopper, and followed their suitcase out of the waiting room, past the ticket office and on out of the station. There, as if they had been transported back two hundred years, stood a horse and cart. The cart was a rough affair, open to the elements, with a driver's seat up front and an apology for a passenger bench behind, and the horse looked in need of several good meals; the contours of its ribs stood out, and it was dwarfed by the heavy shafts of the vehicle it pulled.

By the time Hettie and Tilly emerged from the station, their suitcase had been tossed into the back of the cart and the shopper – prised from Hettie's paws with one swift movement – quickly joined it. Tilly was lifted off her feet and deposited on the passenger bench as Hettie – trying to keep her dignity – scrambled up after her. Their driver wasted no time in springing into his seat, and with a guttural grunt and an encouraging crack of the whip, the horse obligingly retraced its tracks away from the station and onto the moor.

Hettie and Tilly huddled together for warmth, grateful that the driver in front shielded them from the icy blast of wind, which was blowing across the snow covered moor. The howling storm was deafening, and was accompanied by the cracking of ice as giant cartwheels cut through a frozen path which seemed to lead nowhere. How long the two friends clung to each other was hard to say; the extreme cold welded them into a united force, determined to hang on as the cart violently lurched from side to side. Their driver cracked his whip again, this time bringing it down on the horse's back as the animal staggered and slid, giving all its strength to a steep incline. Miraculously, the cart reached the top of the hill and Hettie peered down into the valley to see a sprawl of buildings, black against the snow and as unwelcoming as the worst nightmare.

Their descent was as perilous as the climb and the driver had to engage the large wooden brake several times before they reached the enclave of buildings. The cart rocked through a rough wooden archway into a yard churned up with mud and snow, and came to a sudden standstill. Above her, Hettie could just make out the words 'Jam Makers Inn' on a battered sign which creaked and swung in the wind. She shivered, but this time it was nothing to do with the cold: the bleakness of their situation had come home to her, and the light that glimmered faintly through the window did nothing to assure her that there was a welcome on the other side of the hostelry door. Happily, she was wrong.

The old oak door burst open to reveal a bespectacled,

short, round cat wearing a mop cap tilted to one side and a full-length apron stained with the busyness of life. 'Bless you, what a night to be out! Come in and warm yourselves. Absalom! Lift 'em down – they look frozen solid. And you better get that poor 'orse into 'er stable. She done well to get you 'ere at all.'

Absalom Tweek did as he was told and gathered Hettie and Tilly in his arms. He deposited them just inside the inn and turned back to the cart for their luggage before leading the horse and cart away.

'Now my luvvers, Lamorna Tweek at your service – and that out there is my very own Absalom Tweek. I don't suppose 'e's introduced 'imself as 'e's a cat of few words and most of them don't make much sense to many. Welcome to Jam Makers Inn. Let's 'ave your coats and come through to the fire. I got a nice blaze goin' in the smuggle.'

Hettie and Tilly were completely bewildered. It was as if they had taken the wrong turn at the theatre and ended up on stage in the middle of a pantomime whose narrative nodded to *Mother Goose* and *Treasure Island* with more than a hint of *Dracula*. The friends followed Lamorna Tweek through to what she had described as the 'smuggle' – a dark, low-beamed room lit only by an open fire blazing in a vast grate which took up the whole of one wall. It was hard to see what the rest of the room offered, as the woodsmoke from the fire filled the room. There were settles either side of the fireplace, and

Hettie and Tilly sat on one of them to thaw out whilst the landlady struggled in with their luggage, leaving it at the base of a loft staircase leading up from the bar.

As their hostess bustled out through a door at the back of the bar, Hettie took advantage of her absence to assess their new-found situation. 'What a bloody nightmare!' she began. 'How can any of this be happening? I wouldn't bet against being murdered in our beds if we're foolish enough to climb Lamorna Tweek's stairs – and what sort of a name is that anyway?'

Tilly giggled, more out of nervousness than merriment. 'I suppose it's Cornish, but she does seem quite nice.'

'So was Mrs Lovett before she started putting pastry round Sweeney Tab's customers,' mumbled Hettie as the big oak door banged, signalling the arrival of Absalom Tweek. Lamorna appeared instantly and stood on a crate to help him out of his coat, unwinding the scarf from around his neck and finally removing his weather-beaten hat. Without his outdoor clothing, Absalom Tweek was a sinewy cat with grizzly, patchy fur and no shortage of scars around his face and long neck. His paws were swollen and raw, the fine bones distorted by years of heavy work, and he gave the impression of having been constructed from the worst remains of a neglected graveyard. His clothes hung about him, as if he'd inherited them from a much larger cat, but it was his boots that caught Hettie's and Tilly's attention: they reached from toe to thigh, obscuring his trousers altogether, and were made of fine leather, worthy of any swashbuckler.

Absalom slid onto a stool by the bar in a well-rehearsed movement, and Lamorna put her back into the business of taking his boots off and replacing them with a pair of soft, red slippers. 'There you are, my luvver. Now get them bags up to Damson an' get yourself to the kitchen for your supper – 'tis waitin' for you. I'll see our guests are settled in.' Absalom rose to his full height and lifted the suitcase high onto his shoulder as if it were a cushion, then bumped the tartan shopper up the old staircase behind him.

Lamorna gave her guests her full attention. 'Now, my dears – I got some 'ot soup on my stove and a nice baked loaf with some Cornish Cruncher, and there's a buttered saffron for afters. You can 'ave a glass or two of Doom Bar to wash it down with, if you've a mind.'

Hettie understood very little of what was on offer, but the thought of hot soup and freshly baked bread made her instantly responsive. 'That all sounds very nice. Thank you, Mrs Tweek.'

'Oh call me Lamorna. We don't 'old with fancy titles round 'ere. I'll bring your food dreckly, then we can get you settled in Damson for the night.' Lamorna disappeared, leaving Hettie and Tilly in a slightly more positive frame of mind, although Hettie's remark concerning Mrs Lovett hung a question mark over the contents of the soup.

It seemed an age before Lamorna returned, but it was worth the wait. She appeared through the door at the back of the bar with a tray laden with two bowls of scalding soup and several large chunks of bread. By the time she reached the fire, her glasses had steamed up, rendering her blind, but Hettie rose quickly from the settle to steer both hostess and tray to safe harbour. Lamorna cleaned her spectacles on her apron and returned to her kitchen, leaving them to tuck in to their supper. Any reservations about the contents of the soup were dismissed by both cats after the first mouthful. 'This is the best soup I've ever had,' said Tilly, licking the back of her spoon. 'If it *was* made with dead sea-cats, I wouldn't mind. It's just lovely.'

Hettie had to agree as she wedged a large piece of bread in her mouth, plastered with butter. They had hardly put their spoons down when Lamorna returned with another tray, this time piled high with cheese and what looked like bright yellow currant buns. 'Try some of our Cornish Cruncher,' she said, pointing to the cheese. 'That'll blow your 'ead off, it's so strong – proper cheese, that is. And them's saffron, if you was wondering – buns from Cornish 'eaven. Now, what about a glass of Doom Bar? Best ale in the 'ouse. Good for settling you down on a night like this.'

The very name Doom Bar was enough to put Hettie off, but the delights of Jam Makers Inn had so far proved to be worthy of any first-class 'Pub with

Grub', as Tilly liked to call it, and to refuse the ale of the house might have seemed unfriendly. 'That would be lovely, Lamorna, but two small glasses for us to try might be best, as Tilly and I aren't really drinkers.'

Lamorna sucked in air through her teeth and lifted her apron above her head in shock. 'Not drinkers! And spending the night at Jam Makers? Whatever next!'

Hettie was confused by the unexpected outburst and watched as she bustled round behind the bar and drew off two half-pint mugs of beer from one of the casks lined up on the ledge at the back. Bringing them down with some force on the table by the fire, she pulled up a stool and sat down. 'This 'ere inn 'as secrets that go back 'undreds of years, an' these 'ere walls 'as seen trouble you could only dream of in your worst nightmares – an' the scaaaars remain.' A wide-eyed Tilly sat forward on her settle as Lamorna continued. 'When Absalom and me came 'ere, the place was full of bad, bad cats – murderers, cut-throats, an' even worse.'

Hettie took a large bite from the wedge of cheese she'd cut for herself. As it hit her tongue, she reached for her first sip of Doom Bar to quell the burning sensation, finding time to wonder what could be worse than murderers and cut-throats. She was about to find out, as Lamorna pushed on with her story. 'Long ago, the plague came to the moor an' the folk 'ere protected themselves by shooting any cat that wasn't known to them – in case they got infected, see. Trouble was, they got used to killing strangers, so in the end all that was left was murderers an' ghosts.'

This time it was Tilly who took a sip of Doom Bar, followed by a healthy bite from her saffron bun to take the taste away. Surprisingly, the combination was pleasing and she noticed that even Hettie was making progress with her glass, too. 'Now, killing strangers is no sort of reputation for a wayside inn to 'ave, so no one came 'ere any more except the bad'uns looking for drink an' sport. Fighting to the death, they were, an' these flagstones 'as seen more blood than ale.' Suddenly Lamorna stood and waved her paw to draw their attention to various points of interest. 'Over 'ere, on this very spot, Captain Ludo Stump was cutlassed to the floor an' sliced in four bits. An' Evergreen Flinch breathed 'er laaaast over there by that window, as 'er 'ead was severed from 'er body an' boiled in a pan over that fire you're sitting by. Lankin Tresowes was landlord then, an 'e was 'anged at Truro for stealing sheep an' the murdering of a family up at a big 'ouse Dozeymary Pool way – but 'e came back 'ere to 'aunt the place even though 'e was drawn an' quartered. 'E wanders the moor mostly, but we 'ave seen 'im in the smuggle once or twice round Christmastime. Then there's that beam above your 'ead – cats was chained to that an' roasted by the fire for less than owing a penny or two for beer.'

Lamorna's guided tour was interrupted by the return of her husband, who drew himself a tankard of Doom Bar and made his way over to them. Instantly, she abandoned her lurid tales and dragged a large high-backed carver chair to the fire. Absalom sat down with a grunt of appreciation and proceeded to fill a clay pipe with tobacco. Hettie and Tilly looked on as the landlord settled to his pipe, blowing the finest smoke rings they had ever seen.

Having made sure that Absalom was comfortable, Lamorna turned her attention to settling her guests in for the night. 'If you would care to come with me, I'll get you set up in Damson. It's one of my best rooms, as it 'as a nice view of the moor an' less of a disturbance in the night.'

Tilly and Hettie drained their glasses and stood to follow Lamorna up the stairs, both noticing how light-headed and unsteady they felt, and more than a little fearful of what the night might have in store for them. There were several rooms leading off the landing at the top of the stairs and Damson was straight ahead of them. The others, Hettie noticed, all had one thing in common: jams. The signs on the doors announced a complete set of preserves, from Blackberry and Strawberry to Greengage and Raspberry. Lamorna flung open the door to reveal a small, low-ceilinged room, lit by one oil lamp placed in the window. There were two beds side by side, an old rough oak chest, and a battered basket chair which had seen much better days. The grate in the small fireplace was empty, but the room was pleasantly warm; Hettie could feel the heat rising through cracked and splintered floorboards from the smuggle below. 'I've put you both in 'ere as it's the warmest place to be, and there's more trouble if two rooms is used,' the landlady explained, before adding enigmatically: 'They can't decide which room to 'aunt first, then there's the bangin' and moanin' – goes on all night sometimes.'

'Are you saying that this room is haunted?' asked Hettie, slumping down heavily on one of the beds.

'Why, of course,' Lamorna said, moving towards the door. 'This 'ole place is full of dead cats. You just 'ave to get used to 'em. They go about their business, and if you don't try to interfere with them, then we all rub along nicely together. No need to lock your doors round 'ere, either – they come through the walls. Breakfast is in the smuggle any time after nine. You got a long way to go in the morning, that's if the weather don't come in worse overnight.'

With that as her parting shot, Lamorna Tweek left the room, latching the door behind her. Hettie rose from her bed and bolted it. 'This must be the bleakest place on earth,' she said, as the footsteps faded away. 'How do they stick it out here? They belong in a different century, so what in hell's name are we going to find if we ever reach Crabstock Manor? And is there a connection between Eloise Twinge and the Tweeks?'

'Singe!' said Tilly, before collapsing on the other bed in a Doom-Bar-fuelled fit of uncontrollable giggling.

The laughter was infectious and Hettie made matters worse by attempting to remove her wellingtons by kicking her legs in the air and bouncing on her bed. Both cats had lost control, and, after a long day fraught with problems and the prospect of a spectre-filled night at Jam Makers Inn, they collapsed exhausted into a deep sleep. Not even the headless spirit of Evergreen Flinch could wake them as she searched through their luggage in the early dawn, scattering the tartan shopper's remaining greaseproof parcels all over their floor.

# CHAPTER SEVEN

Tilly woke first. She pulled a blanket from her bed and wrapped it around herself before padding across the boards to the window. It was hard to see beyond the glass, as the snow lay thickly across the small panes. She lifted the catch and, with a push, the window swung open, letting in an icy blast. After the smoky rooms at the Inn, the fresh, cold air was a real tonic and Tilly lifted her face to it, breathing in the complete whiteout of the landscape that stretched before her. In the far distance, she noticed a contrasting band of dark grey, and her heart leapt as she realised that it was the sea.

So enthralled was she at the vision before her that she didn't notice Hettie by her side until she spoke. 'Well, we might be in the middle of nowhere, held up in a pub and neck deep in snow, but I have to admit this beats most of the cases we've been called in for – and we haven't even started the investigation yet.' Hettie turned away from the window and suddenly noticed the state of the floor. 'What on earth have you been looking for?'

Tilly turned from the window, pulling it shut behind her, and stared at the floor. 'It wasn't me – not unless I was sleepwalking.' She gathered the food parcels up and placed them carefully back in the tartan shopper. 'Look – the suitcase has been opened, too.'

Hettie cast her eye across its contents. 'Nothing missing as far as I can see, but it's a bit of a mess. Maybe Lamorna Tweek's permanent guests have been going about their business. The door's still bolted, so they didn't come in by any normal route – if there *is* anything normal about Jam Makers Inn.' The unmistakable smell of bacon began to rise through the holes in Damson's floorboards, which could only mean one thing. 'Breakfast!' said Hettie, roughly tidying the suitcase and deciding to remain in the clothes she had travelled and slept in. 'We'd better get our stuff together before we go down.'

Tilly pulled on her wellingtons, buttoned up her cardigan, parked the shopper by the door and followed Hettie downstairs to the smuggle. The bar was thick with woodsmoke, billowing out in thick plumes from the fireplace, so they chose a table by the window, hoping for more light and a little less smoke. A loud banging of pots and pans came from the room behind the bar, and Hettie was just about to announce their arrival when Lamorna Tweek bustled through to greet them. 'Good morning! I 'ope you 'ad a restful night. 'Tis bad news about your onward journey – there's no chance of getting away across the moor today. Blocked solid, and no chance of it meltin' till tomorrow. We 'ad another big fall of it in the night, and Absalom is diggin' the 'orse out of 'er stable so we can feed 'er, poor old thing. We rescued 'er last spring from a bad old cat who treated 'er rough, and we 'as to keep feedin' 'er cause she got so thin. What will it be for breakfast? I got bacon, scrumbled eggs, sausages and a Doom Bar potato cake – that's me normal breakfast, although I could run to a chop if you prefer.'

Hettie and Tilly beamed at their landlady, almost pleased not to be going anywhere. 'Two normal breakfasts would be lovely,' said Hettie, ordering for them both. 'But I was wondering what scrumbled eggs might be?'

Lamorna laughed. 'Scrumbled eggs! Tha's just how I do 'em. I don't mix 'em proper, so you get bits of cooked white along with the yellow – more like a poached egg gone wrong, really, but I makes 'em with lots of butter.'

'Then scrumbled eggs it is,' said Hettie decisively,

wishing they had booked in to Jam Makers Inn for the whole of Christmas.

The breakfast, when it came, was well worth waiting for. As she wiped the butter from her chin and mopped up the bacon fat with her last forkful of Doom Bar potato, Tilly pointed out that she would prefer her eggs to be scrumbled from that day forward, and Hettie had to agree that it was probably the best breakfast she had ever eaten. Whatever the rest of the day might hold, it had begun on a high note.

Lamorna returned for the empty plates and – as was her custom – sat to pass the time of day with her guests, bringing an empty tea cup with her. Before she had a chance to point out any more death sites on her flagstone floor, Hettie felt it was time for a little fact-gathering of her own. 'Lamorna – what can you tell us about Crabstock Manor?'

'Well, the short answer is 'ow long 'ave you got?' said the landlady, settling in and pouring herself a cup of tea from Hettie and Tilly's pot. 'Lady Crabstock-Singe – she's the last one of that family, and all them that came before 'ave been murdered since the doin' away of Christmas Paws.'

'Christmas Paws?' repeated Hettie, trying to hang on to what she suspected was going to be one of Lamorna's elaborate presentations. 'Is that some kind of seasonal ritual?'

'Bless you, no,' responded Lamorna with a chuckle.

'Christmas Paws was a young servant cat. She worked in the kitchens at Crabstock Manor a long time past, and the story goes that the young Lord Crabstock took a fancy to 'er an' used 'er in such a way that she fell for some kittens. She 'ad 'igh 'opes of bein' the lady of the manor, but when 'e found out she was carrying 'e turned 'er out and set 'is dogs to chasin' 'er. She ran and she ran till she came to the cliff's edge, but there was no escapin' them dogs so she fell off the cliff and bounced twenty times on the rocks before 'er poor broken body was swallowed by the sea, along with the kittens she was carryin'. The young Lord Crabstock, 'appy with 'is day's work, returned to the manor, sayin' that Christmas 'ad run off – but that was just the start of the troubles.'

Lamorna took a sip of her tea, giving Hettie a chance to comment. 'Why did Christmas Paws have to die? He could have just sent her away.'

'Ah well – she knew secrets, see. She knew that young Lord Crabstock wasn't who 'e thought 'e was. 'Is mother, the Dowager Crabstock, 'ad taken a fancy to Pullet Crop, the cat that looked after the chickens on the estate. So 'e was born the other side of the 'en 'ouse if you know what I mean, and poor Christmas tried to blackmail 'im into making 'er the lady of Crabstock. So she 'ad to go, really. Silly cat.'

Hettie agreed that it was a sorry mess, but failed to see why they had been called in to deal with an old crime that was clearly typical of its age. 'What has all this to do with Lady Eloise Crabstock-Twinge?'

'Singe!' corrected Tilly.

'As far as I can tell,' Lamorna continued, 'the ghost of Christmas Paws 'as been seen up at the manor, and she been leavin' messages in the flour.'

'In the garden?' asked Tilly, intrigued.

'No, my dear – in the flour left over from rollin' the pastry in the kitchen.'

'What sort of messages?' asked Hettie, trying to stifle the laugh that was rising in her throat.

'Things like "You're next!" and "Death to the Crabstocks!" – which is a bit odd, as Christmas Paws wasn't known for formin' 'er letters. Servants didn't read nor write in them times.'

'It sounds like a practical joke to me,' said Hettie.

Lamorna smiled. 'Not much of a joke when your 'ole family 'as been wiped out. Lady Eloise 'ad two brothers and a sister, all murdered in the worst of ways, and always after Christmas's ghost 'as appeared up at the manor. That's why she wants you to take it on before she's murdered, too. Sooner we can get you to Crabstock, the more chance she 'as of survivin' the festive season.'

'How do you know about all this? Is it one of those Cornish legends?'

Lamorna stood up and began to pile the licked-clean breakfast pots onto a tray. 'That story 'as been in my family for a long time. Christmas Paws is sort of one of them distant relations. She was a cousin of the Bunns, and that's my family name, see. The Bunns 'as always served the Crabstocks up at the manor. I started in the kitchens there, and I would 'ave stayed 'ad it not been for me bein' swept off me paws by Absalom Tweek. 'E came to me with gold in 'is pockets from one of 'is sea voyages and said 'e'd like to set up with me, so the Crabstocks let me go and we ended up at Jam Makers. My brother, Hevva, and his long-term "live-in", Saffron, still looks after the place for Lady Crabstock, so you'll be meetin' them soon enough.'

'How will we get to Crabstock Manor?' asked Hettie, thinking about the poor state of the Tweeks' rescued horse.

'Well, we was 'opin that Marlon Brandish, the post-cat, could take you on from 'ere in 'is van, but 'e won't be getting through today so you'll 'ave to amuse yourselves. Absalom's cuttin' a Christmas tree for the smuggle later, so we can get done up, and I'm roastin' a nice bit of beef for your supper.'

Tilly was very pleased to be staying an extra day at Jam Makers Inn. It seemed the sort of place that needed exploring, and when the two friends returned to their room after breakfast, she wasted no time in selecting an array of outdoor clothes suitable for a foray onto the snow-bound moor. 'I think my cardigan with a hood and an extra pair of socks in my wellingtons should keep the frost off,' she said, 'and I'm doubling up on my mittens, too.'

Hettie couldn't help but smile as Tilly grew and grew in size with each new layer of clothes; by the time they made their way downstairs to face the elements, she could hardly move at all, so constricted was she by swathes of hand-knits. The final straw was her greatcoat; she couldn't bend her arms sufficiently to fit into the sleeves, and it took much tugging and pulling before they were finally ready to face Bodkin Moor.

Hettie pulled the huge oak door open and immediately shielded her eyes from the extreme light that greeted them. The overnight snow had created a perfect carpet in the inn's yard, untouched except for one set of paw prints which led away from the door and over to a clutch of single storey buildings. A mountain of snow was piled high outside the building nearest to them, and Absalom Tweek stood with spade in paw, satisfied that the door to his stable was now free of obstruction. Seeing his guests emerge from the inn, he nodded before lifting the bar on the stable door and disappearing inside to be greeted by a grateful whiney.

'Where shall we go first?' asked Tilly enthusiastically. 'It's all so pretty.'

'I don't think we should go very far,' said Hettie, buttoning her coat. 'And we should keep the inn in sight all the time. We're strangers in a very isolated place.'

Tilly giggled. 'Oh, that's very funny – ICE-OLATED! That's a good joke.'

It took Hettie a moment to appreciate Tilly's play on words, but once the penny had dropped the two cats set off in a merry mood to explore the immediate area of Jam Makers Inn. The buildings were low to the ground and nestled in a valley seemingly devoid of any vegetation; the surrounding hills boasted a ridge of trees that stood like phantoms, dark and motionless with their black twisted branches all reaching out in the same direction, blasted by storms that rolled in from the sea. The cart track that served as the main road to and from the inn was no longer visible, and it was only the rough wooden arch that gave a hint to where the path lay under the night's heavy fall of snow.

'Not sure that Marlon Brandish and his van will get through this lot tomorrow,' observed Hettie, scraping a mittenful of snow from a fence post; she formed a perfect snowball and tossed it high into the air, stepping aside as it returned to earth, narrowly missing her.

'Let's build a snow cat,' suggested Tilly, forming her own snowball and rolling it along the ground until it was almost half her size. Hettie joined in, and the body of the snow cat was soon ready for a head; she started the new snowball while Tilly scrabbled in the snow for stones and twigs to use as features. Eventually the creature was finished, and such a fine specimen of ice sculpture has never been seen on Bodkin Moor before or since. The cat stood tall, glistening in a pale, wintery sun which had just burst from the snow clouds that hung so thickly in the sky. His whiskers were twisted twigs, his ears pyramids of compacted ice, and, when dark stones were added for eyes and nose, the snow cat seemed to take on a life of his own; in fact, there was a moment when Tilly thought he'd actually winked at her.

'Come on,' said Hettie, dusting the snow from her mittens. 'Let's walk for a bit to keep warm.'

Tilly stood for a moment in silent conversation with the snow cat. 'He'd like to be called Osbert Twigg,' she said eventually, 'with a double "g".'

Hettie admired her friend's choice of name. 'Well, Osbert Twigg with a double "g" it is, then.'

# CHAPTER EIGHT

The snow was too deep to go far on the moor, but the fresh air was bracing and Hettie and Tilly confined themselves to the inn's immediate outskirts. The sun was beginning to melt the snow underfoot, and the mix of slush and mud made their progress slow. By the time they reached the other side of the sprawl of buildings, they'd had enough and decided to make their way back to the smoky comfort of the smuggle bar. They looked in on the stable to find the Tweeks' horse bathed in lantern light and mountains of straw, chewing its way through a nosebag of oats fit for an animal three times its size. Hettie couldn't help but think that it had well and truly landed on its hooves the day Absalom Tweek led it away from the abuse of its former life.

Next to the stable was another building of similar size. Without thinking, Hettie pushed the door open and immediately wished with all her heart that she hadn't. The two cats stared in absolute horror at what was before them. On a bench in the middle of the room was a very dead cat, splayed out and pinned by each of its paws to a board; its empty eye sockets stared back at Hettie and Tilly, who stood frozen to the spot on the threshold of some sort of torture chamber. As well as the dead cat, the bench displayed a number of evil looking implements: a set of large needles; coils of wire; a jar of slimy liquid with a brush sticking out of it; and worst of all, a set of scalpels, lined up in order of size. 'We need to get out of here as soon as we can,' said Hettie, backing away from the door. 'We'll pretend we haven't seen anything, pack our stuff together, and get going before it gets dark.'

Tilly looked across to the inn and was horrified to see Absalom Tweek bearing down on them. 'I think we need to get going now!'

They took off in the direction of the open moor and ran blindly through the snow with Absalom Tweek hot on their heels, shouting and waving his paws as he gained on them. Hettie's heart pounded in her chest as she ran for her life. Looking back to make sure that Tilly was keeping up, she was just in time to hear her friend cry out as she was swallowed up in the snow. Absalom Tweek was quickly upon her, and Hettie turned and flew at the innkeeper, hoping to give Tilly time to get to her feet, but he sidestepped her assault, pushing her into the snow. Dazed and frightened, Hettie struggled to her feet as Absalom Tweek tore off his coat; Tilly was nowhere to be seen, and Hettie realised suddenly that she had fallen down a hole. Tweek wasted no time in climbing into the chasm after her, and all Hettie could do was stand rooted to the spot, terrified of what might happen next.

Tilly's cries didn't last long. The sudden silence told Hettie that her friend had been quickly despatched at the paws of Absalom Tweek. He emerged from the hole in the snow, carrying her body in his arms, and Hettie let out a sob that echoed across the moor. She would be next, but she didn't care; there was no point in running, and the thought of leaving Tilly in such a godforsaken place was beyond her. Tweek grabbed his coat from the snow and bundled Tilly's body into it, throwing it over his shoulder before striding back to the inn. Hettie followed, the silent witness to her friend's murder.

Lamorna Tweek was waiting at the inn door, no less welcoming than usual. 'Come in by the fire, my dears, and we'll see what's to be done.'

Absalom carried his bundle to the fireplace and Hettie watched as Tilly was laid out on the hearth rug, her greatcoat soaked and one of her best striped winter socks revealed where she had lost a wellington.

It was a moment before she realised that Lamorna was shouting at her. 'Come on! Let's get 'er clothes off so them flames can get at 'er.' Hettie stared in horror as the Tweeks ripped and tore at Tilly's clothes and Lamorna began to pound her chest. 'Don't just stand there! Look, we got 'er breathin' again. Come and see to 'er while I get a blanket – and Absalom, get a tot of your best brandy.'

Hettie ran to the fireplace as Tilly gradually regained her hold on the world around her. A violent bout of sneezing finally brought her to her senses, encouraged by a hot trickle of brandy down her throat. She sat up as Lamorna wrapped a blanket round her. 'Dear me, whatever were you two doing out on the moor in this weather? Them old mine shafts 'ave claimed no end of cats. You was lucky Absalom was about.'

Hettie wondered whether she should explain the circumstances of their hasty exit from the confines of the yard; the slam of the big oak door, signalling Absalom's departure, made her mind up for her. 'The thing is,' she began, 'we've discovered a nasty secret about Mr Tweek and we were running away from him when Tilly fell down the hole.' As Hettie listened to her own words, she began to question the truth of them; the realisation that Absalom had saved Tilly's life was at odds with the accusation she was about to make, and she changed course just in time. 'Actually,' she continued, 'I'm not sure what happened, but we saw something in one of the buildings that frightened us.'

'Cat stuffing!' said Lamorna, throwing her head back in a raucous laugh. 'Absalom's famous round 'ere for 'is "Tabby Tableaux", as I likes to call 'em. Nothin' for you to be frightened of. Folks bring their dear departed from all over Cornwall to 'ave them immortalised in 'is little scenes. 'E does a lovely job on 'em, and once a year we 'ave a big display 'ere at Jam Makers – cats come from all over to buy 'em. 'Is glass cases 'as travelled the world, and 'e's never short of cats to stuff. We stores 'em in an ice 'ouse at the back of the stable till 'e can get round to 'em.'

Hettie found Lamorna's matter-of-fact way of describing Absalom's hobby a little disturbing, but – after her recent fears – she was almost joyous to know that there was an ice house full of corpses waiting to be gutted and restitched by the landlord.

Tilly was looking much better. Satisfied that her patient had rallied, Lamorna gathered up her wet clothes. 'I'll 'ave to get these all dried out over my kitchen range, and I got to get my beef on for your dinners. I'll bring you some 'ot soup in a while, but you listen 'ere – my Absalom is the kindest cat you'll ever know. 'E'd never 'urt an 'air on your 'ead, and when you're feelin' stronger I'll get 'im to show you some of 'is works. We got 'em in the Tinners Retreat through there.' Lamorna pointed to a door in the far corner of the smuggle, and – leaving Hettie and Tilly feeling rather stupid – went about her work.

'I'm a bit under dressed,' said Tilly, struggling to her feet. 'I think I should go and find some dry clothes.' She made a few shaky steps towards the stairs before Hettie took her arm, and they climbed the stairs together, hoping for a little peace and quiet in the sanctuary of their room. Damson was very quiet, but the state of the floor and beds suggested that a whirlwind had passed through very recently. Blankets were strewn about the room, the tartan shopper lay upside down with its wheels in the air, and their suitcase had emptied its contents in a heaped-up pile by the window. 'Do you think we should say something?' asked Tilly, surveying the chaos.

'I think we should tidy up and pretend it hasn't happened,' said Hettie firmly, gathering up the blankets and throwing them back onto the beds. 'We've already accused the landlord of trying to murder us. I think if we start coming up with a list of complaints about our room we could be out on our ears. Maybe this is Lamorna's idea of room service.' Tilly giggled, which instantly brought on a bout of coughing. 'Come on – let's get you into some warm clothes,' Hettie continued, pulling out a cardigan and a pair of woolly socks from the pile by the window. 'When you're dressed we'll go back down and sit by the fire till the soup comes.'

She did her best to repack the suitcase and turn the shopper the right way up, taking care not to disturb too many of the Butters' greaseproof parcels. The salmon turnovers were beginning to look a bit worse for wear, so the two cats made short work of them as an appetiser before the meal which awaited them on a table by the fire in the smuggle.

# CHAPTER NINE

The day passed without any further excitement. Tilly dozed by the fire after her ordeal, and Hettie read aloud to her from a book she'd found abandoned on the settle, clearly one of Lamorna's: *Haunted Inns of Cornwall* by Demelza Wince. There was a whole chapter on Jam Makers Inn, and most of it was taken up with the sorry tale of Evergreen Flinch, who was said to rifle through the guests rooms looking for her head. Hettie was still pondering the story when the big oak door flew open and a giant Christmas tree appeared, followed by Absalom Tweek, who dragged the spruce across to the window of the smuggle. Lamorna bustled through from her kitchen with a bucket of soil, and the landlord and his lady secured the tree and stood back to admire it. Absalom grunted with satisfaction and

Lamorna clapped her paws together in sheer delight. 'Well done, my luvver! I think it's the best tree you've ever cut.' She beamed at Hettie and Tilly. 'Would you two like to 'elp with the decorations? I got a big box of sparkly things to put on it.'

Tilly, now fully awake, responded immediately. 'Oooh! Yes please. That would be a lovely thing to do.'

Pleased to see Tilly looking so much better, Lamorna dragged a large box from behind the bar. 'There you go. You get crackin' – I've got to baste my meat. When you've finished the tree you can 'ave a look at Absalom's tableaux.'

Hettie and Tilly set about the box of decorations, choosing from coloured glass baubles in a range of sizes and clipping small metal holders to the ends of the branches, ready for Absalom to fill with twisted candles. Eventually there was only one thing left in the box: a large silver star. Tilly turned the decoration over in her paws and, without warning, Absalom swept her up in his arms and lifted her to the top of the tree to place the star. When she had been returned gently to the floor, the three cats stood back to admire their work: the tree had summoned in the season well and truly, and it filled the smuggle at Jam Makers Inn with the magical expectation of Christmas.

With perfect timing, Lamorna burst through from her kitchen bearing a plate piled high with hot sausage rolls. Absalom filled four small tot glasses with his best cherry brandy and the small assembled company raised their glasses to the festive season. Lamorna returned to her baking, allowing herself a couple of verses of 'God Rest Ye Merry Gentlemen' as the Christmas spirit engulfed her, and Absalom grunted to the room next door by way of an invitation to view his work. Hettie felt obliged to show some interest in his macabre hobby as she had spent most of the day calling him a murderer, so she made suitably appreciative noises and followed, dragging Tilly along by her cardigan.

The room was much bigger than the smuggle, low beamed and better equipped to handle a considerable amount of passing trade during the summer months. There were tables, stools and benches everywhere, and the bar that served the room shone with horse brasses and lanterns; miniature galleons sailed between the bottles nestled in their optics, interspersed with other seafaring objects obligatory to the Cornish holiday trade, but it was the glass presentation cases around the walls that stole the show. Hettie and Tilly gasped in unison at the sight before them, and Absalom nodded with satisfaction and returned to the smuggle, leaving the two friends to conduct their own guided tour.

'I've never seen anything so lovely,' said Tilly, staring at a display which featured a string quartet.

'Just look at them – they're perfect. You can almost hear the music.'

Although they were looking at four dead cats, dressed in white tie and tails and posed with instruments, Hettie had to agree that the overall effect was one of wonder and fascination. 'Look at this one!' she said, marvelling at the sight before her. 'It's a schoolroom full of kittens. They've all got slates and chalk, and one of them's holding an old ink pen. That teacher – he's a big old cat!'

She found it difficult to pull herself away from the scene before her, but Tilly was in raptures at another. 'And here! It's a kittens' tea party. There must be at least ten of them. Look at those two pouring the tea and going round with the milk jug. It's as if they're putting on a play for us.'

Hettie and Tilly worked their way round the room, staring in amazement at Absalom Tweek's display boxes – a perfect depiction of everyday life, except for one thing. 'It's the eyes I have a problem with,' observed Hettie, taking a closer look at the final case in which a gathering of cats was huddled round a coffin; the lid was open to reveal an elderly tabby with her paws crossed over her chest. 'That's what gives them away – the eyes are dead. They just stare out at you with nothing behind them.'

Tilly thought for a moment and looked back at some of the other cases. 'I suppose that's because they *are* all dead,' she said, returning to admire the string quartet. 'The thing is – what if you don't like the case you're put in? That cat playing the violin probably didn't even know the one playing the cello, and none of us wants to go to a tea party with kittens we don't get on with.'

Hettie acknowledged the problem. 'The very thought of spending eternity trapped in a glass case at a kittens' tea party would fill me with such dread that I would have to come back and haunt whoever did it,' she said. 'No wonder Jam Makers Inn has so many unwelcome guests swirling about the place.'

The room was cold and Tilly shivered. It had been a strange couple of days, where life and death had hung in the balance, and their original reason for coming to Cornwall felt like a distant memory: they were still a long way from getting started on the Crabstock Manor Case. Darkness had fallen outside, but the occasional thud of snow as it slipped from the roof suggested that a thaw was underway; they would soon be able to leave Jam Makers Inn and move on to the village of Porthladle and the mystery surrounding the ghost of Christmas Paws.

The smuggle looked warm and welcoming after the bleakness of the other bar. Absalom had lit several lanterns and dotted them about, and the fire was roaring in the grate, giving light to the whole room. One of the long tables had been moved to the centre of the floor and Lamorna was busy laying it up for four. 'Come on, you two! I thought I'd make your last night a bit of an occasion, it bein' almost Christmas. We can all sit down together now we're proper friends. Absalom's haulin' the beef out of the oven, and everything else will be ready dreckly. Snow's meltin', so you should get through to Crabstock tomorrow. Weather's bad there on account of the storms, but Marlon will get you there right enough.'

Hettie was beginning to wonder whether there was ever a good time to travel across Cornwall and viewed the prospect of Marlon and his van with very little confidence, but tonight they were warm, safe and reasonably content, and the prospect of sharing a large joint of roast beef in front of a blazing fire and a Christmas tree was enough to make a cat's heart sing – and sing they did, but that was much later.

While preparations for the dinner continued in the smuggle, Hettie and Tilly returned to their room to change, wanting to look their best for their hosts. Much to their relief, Evergreen Flinch had not continued her search through their luggage for her head – if, indeed, it had been Evergreen Flinch – and all was as they had left it. Hettie selected a pair of her best business slacks and a stripy jumper to match, completing the look with a waistcoat. Tilly – keen to give a festive flavour to her outfit – chose a purple cardigan with yellow buttons and a pair of lime green socks with red toes. Ready for their evening, the two cats made their way back downstairs just in time to see Absalom carrying the biggest piece of beef they had ever seen to the table. The smell filled their nostrils, and Tilly wiped a dribble from her chin with the sleeve of her cardigan as her mouth watered with anticipation.

The table groaned with food. Besides the beef, there were hot Cornish pasties, tiny sausages rolled in bacon, small chicken pies, and a curious-looking dish of puff pastry with four fish heads sticking out of the top of it. Tilly approached it with caution, wondering if it was one of Absalom's works of art, and Lamorna noticed her interest. 'That there is a Stargazy Pie,' she explained. 'I always makes one round Christmastime, as close to the anniversary as I can get. It should be the 23rd by rights, but as we 'ave visitors I thought you'd like a proper taste of Cornwall.'

'What sort of anniversary is it?' asked Tilly, giving the fish a closer inspection.

'Ah, well. The story comes from the village of Mousehole, and the pie is to 'onour a brave fishercat who went by the name of Tom Bawcock. 'E sailed out in a violent storm to catch fish to save the villagers from starvation. 'E come ashore with seven different types which they made into a giant pie that got shared out, savin' them from the famine, and 'e became an 'ero of sorts. Every 23rd of December, they makes a big Stargazy Pie to remember 'im by.'

'So are there seven types of fish in this?' Hettie asked, joining in.

'Oh no. I just use pilchards to decorate, really, although Absalom is partial to a good chew on them fish 'eads after I've cut into it.'

There was an appreciative grunt from the end of the table as Absalom set about the joint of beef with a large, long-bladed knife which he had spent some time sharpening while Lamorna told her story. Tilly was now fascinated by the pie. 'What else have you put in it?'

Lamorna answered by breaking into the pie with a fish slice. 'You look 'ere. That's potato, that layer is 'ard-boiled eggs, then comes me pastry, an' pilchards to finish.'

Hettie couldn't resist commenting. 'If they were starving, where did they get the potatoes, eggs and the stuff to make the pastry from?'

Lamorna laughed. 'Well, you do 'ave a point there. It's not something I've thought about much, but it's a good excuse for a festive pie right enough.'

It was a jolly evening, and both Hettie and Tilly were surprised to find themselves in such good company. When they could eat no more, Absalom pulled the table away from the fire, lit the Christmas tree candles and returned with a jug of Doom Bar,

75

which he warmed by thrusting a hot poker into its depths. Hettie, Tilly and Lamorna settled themselves in front of the flames and Absalom completed the quartet by falling into his fireside chair. He filled a clay pipe from a jar of catnip, and passed it to his wife. 'Will you take a pipe?' he mumbled, looking across at Hettie, and selecting another pipe from a brass pot by his chair.

She hesitated, slightly concerned by how strong Cornish catnip might be. Lamorna seemed to be puffing away without any obvious effect, though, so caution was once again thrown to the wind. 'That would be lovely,' she said.

The catnip turned out to be the lesser of two evils. Hettie had forgotten to factor in the mug of warm Doom Bar as she blew smoke rings into the fire, and it was a mercy that Tilly touched neither; she fell asleep in her fireside chair shortly after dinner, making her the only entirely sober cat at the inn that night, and was eventually woken by an impromptu fireside carol concert. Hettie had been armed with a battered old guitar and was playing 'In The Bleak Midwinter', accompanied by Lamorna on vocals and spoons and Absalom on washboard. The song session continued for some time, and even Tilly was pressed into singing a sweet and tuneful 'Away in a Manger' from the middle of the dining table, bringing a tear to Absalom's good eye as she did so.

To say that Hettie, Lamorna and Absalom had to crawl up the stairs would be an understatement, and if Tilly hadn't helped Hettie out of her clothes and into her bed, things could have been much worse in the morning.

It was a little before dawn when Tilly awoke to the sound of their suitcase being opened, as the spectre of Evergreen Flinch twirled around the room minus her head.

# CHAPTER TEN

If Evergreen had been doomed for eternity, Hettie would have gladly changed places with her when she woke that morning. Her head ached from the tips of her ears to the bottom of her chin, and the rhythmic throbbing behind her eyeballs gave her every good reason to want to lie down and die. She sat up in bed and was instantly sick into a chamber pot that Tilly had anticipated would be needed.

Tilly's cheerful nature was something that Hettie had always admired; it had seen them through some scrapes in the past, but today, as she flitted around their room clearing up after Evergreen and humming various tunes of the season, her exuberance was the worst torture imaginable. The smell of fried bacon rising up through the floorboards wasn't helping, either, but it served as a reminder that today they must continue their journey to Crabstock Manor; a good breakfast was sure to help them on their way.

Hettie struggled from her bed, gingerly putting one paw in front of the other until she reached their neatly packed suitcase. Tilly did her best not to laugh at the extreme state her friend was in, and came to the rescue as she stared in bewilderment down at the clothes. 'I've chosen for you, and I've gone for warm but comfortable.' Hettie followed the direction of Tilly's paw, and there at the bottom of her bed were her travel clothes, laid out ready for her to climb into.

With Tilly's help, and after several failed attempts at putting on her wellingtons, Hettie was ready to face the day. The two cats made their way down to the smuggle, where Lamorna was holding court at the bar with a rotund cat squeezed into a bright red uniform which had seen better days. 'Ah! There you are, my dears,' she bellowed. 'Come and meet Marlon. 'E'll be takin' you on to Crabstock Manor when you've 'ad your breakfast.'

Hettie was instantly beset by a bout of dizziness and had to sit down on the first stool she almost fell over. Tilly continued forward to shake the portly paw of Marlon, who beamed and winked at her like a long-lost uncle. 'Pleased to make your acquaintance an' I'm most 'onoured to be deliverin' you safe an' sound to Crabstock,' he said, before downing what was left of his pint of Doom Bar. Tilly couldn't help but think that the sooner they got on the road the more likely they were to arrive safe and sound, but Lamorna replenished his glass.

Feeling able to stand again, Hettie made slow progress to the table by the window which was laid up for breakfast. Tilly sat opposite her and they waited for Lamorna to take their order, but she was still busy at the bar: having pulled another pint for the post-cat, she set about making what looked like a rather evil cocktail, and Tilly watched in admiration as she flew up and down the optics with a tumbler – rum, gin, whisky, then, worst of all, Tabasco and a whole raw egg. She held her breath as Lamorna took a large spoon to the mix, but, instead of drinking it, the landlady emerged from behind the bar and slammed the tumbler down in front of Hettie. 'There you go – get that down you in one an' you'll be as right as rain by the time I bring you your full Cornish!'

Lamorna didn't wait to see Hettie drink her potion, but shot through her kitchen door like a cat on a mission. Marlon swivelled round on his bar stool, giving his full attention to Hettie and Tilly's table. 'Come on, then,' he coaxed. 'On the count of three – one, two, three!'

Hettie had no idea why she felt the need to respond to Marlon Brandish's encouragement, but she forced the brown slimy mixture down her throat. It was touch and go for a second, but her self-control had to be admired and the hangover cure stayed where it was, earning her a round of applause from Tilly and Marlon. By the time Lamorna returned with two full Cornish breakfasts, Hettie was feeling much better; the nausea had disappeared and the headache was receding to a manageable irritation.

The cats cleaned their plates as Marlon soaked up some of his – now three – pints of Doom Bar with a giant bacon, sausage and chicken bap. Wiping the grease from several chins, he rolled off his bar stool. 'I'll go an' fire up my van, an' you come out when you're ready. We should be at Crabstock before dark if we get on soon. There's more weather comin' in overnight so you'll need to be tucked up before it hits.' With that, Marlon Brandish left the smuggle and banged the big oak door shut behind him.

'I wonder what he meant by "before it hits",' mused Hettie, piling up their empty plates. 'I get the feeling that Crabstock Manor isn't very high up on the places-to-visit list.'

'We thought that about Jam Makers Inn, but it's been just lovely here,' Tilly said, buttoning up the travel cardigan that Lamorna had successfully dried out after her fall down the mineshaft; Absalom had gone to great pains, too, to retrieve her missing wellington from the hole in the snow. 'It's a shame we've got to leave today. I'd love to spend Christmas here – we had such a jolly time last night.'

The memory of her overindulgence inspired Hettie to change the subject before she revisited her breakfast. 'We'd better make tracks,' she said. 'I'll go and fetch the suitcase down if you can manage the tartan shopper, then we'd better say our farewells and throw ourselves on the mercy of Marlon and his van.'

Evergreen Flinch had resisted the temptation to disrupt their luggage, and it was with some regret that they closed the door on Damson and bumped down the stairs and out into what was now a very muddy yard. True to his word, Marlon had his engine running, but, as Hettie looked over the bright red vehicle, an air of uncertainty engulfed her: the engine sounded like it had been modified for a tractor and the actual bodywork still clinging to the chassis of the small van was sporadic; there was a wheel arch missing from the front, and the number plate was tied on at a jaunty angle, dangling in the mud at the back where one of the doors had suffered some sort of impact. She glanced across the yard at the stable where Absalom's rescue horse was devouring a nosebag of oats, and wished with all her heart that their onward journey to Crabstock Manor could be achieved in the same manner as they had arrived. Seeing her hesitation, Marlon leapt from his driver's seat and took charge of the luggage, hurling it into the back of the van in case she changed her mind; Lady Crabstock offered him a handsome fee for transporting her guests from Jam Makers Inn, and he wasn't about to jeopardise that.

'There's room for you both up front,' the post-cat said as he secured the back doors with a length of rope. 'Best to share a seat close to the 'eater as it won't reach the back.'

Hettie and Tilly struggled through the mud to the passenger side of Marlon's van and eyed up the space they were to share. As they were about to get in, Absalom strode across the yard, waving towards the archway. They looked in the direction to which he pointed and noticed that their carefully constructed snow cat, Osbert Twigg, now wore one of his old wide-brimmed hats and a red-and-green striped scarf, and stood waiting to wave them off. Lamorna joined Absalom in the yard and thrust a warm parcel into Hettie's paws. ''Ot pasties just out of my oven for your journey. Make sure you both come back an' see us very soon.' Absalom grunted in agreement and Hettie and Tilly climbed into Marlon's van and settled themselves amid a sea of empty Doom Bar bottles and crisp packets.

Marlon revved up the van and released the handbrake, setting the back wheels spinning in the mud and splattering Lamorna and Absalom from head to toe. Now that both the landlord and his lady were as filthy as they could be, there was no reason why they shouldn't pitch in to release the van from its quagmire – and pitch in they did, using every ounce of strength they could muster until the van finally broke free of the mud and shot across the yard and out through the archway.

The rear-view mirror revealed an endearing image of Lamorna and Absalom Tweek, lying prostrate in the mud and lifting their paws in unison in a final act of hospitality as they waved their visitors off across Bodkin Moor. In fact, Tilly could have sworn that even Osbert Twigg smiled and nodded as they spun past him.

# CHAPTER ELEVEN

The moor was still deep in snow and the tracks remained hazardous, although it was clear to Hettie and Tilly that Marlon Brandish was master of this wild terrain, with or without his Doom Bar habit. The van rose and fell with every dip and bump in the road, slipping and sliding first on the ice and then on the mud; eventually, as the winter sun rose in the sky, Marlon forced his way through perilously deep floods of melted snow.

The van may have seen better days, but sadly there was nothing wrong with the cassette machine which poked its way out of the dashboard. Marlon's passion for Cornish choirs didn't sit too well with Hettie's or Tilly's ears for a good tune, and by the time they left the moors behind and were heading for the south coast, they would both have been thrilled to set Trelawny free by taking up the good sword and a trusty paw themselves. It was no surprise that this Cornish cat of legend had been imprisoned in the Tower of London if he sang in the same aggressive manner as the Rinsey Tom Cat Ensemble, who had been delighting and disturbing in equal measure since the journey began.

It occurred to Hettie that a little light conversation might serve as good reason to turn down the in-van entertainment, and, after a bit of a shouting match, Marlon's paw reached for the volume control. Relieved not to have to sit through 'Bread of Heaven' one more time – it was clearly one of Marlon's top tunes – Hettie launched into a series of questions which she thought he might enjoy answering. Almost by accident, Tilly hit the eject button on the cassette, allowing the Rinsey choir to leap into the footwell along with the empty Doom Bar bottles; it was a perfect example of teamwork, and the journey continued in a slightly more peaceful fashion.

'Do you have any deliveries to do today?' Hettie asked, noticing that there was no postbag in the van.

'Not as such,' Marlon replied, crunching his gears. 'I tries to limit the hours I'm out at this time of year – on account of the weather, see. We gets snow on the moors an' storms on the shores, an' all sorts in between, an' my poor van an' me suffer from the weather. We don't come out unless there's a proper job on.'

Hettie thought for a moment, staring at Marlon's crumpled uniform and mentally comparing his lacklustre approach to that of their own postmistress, Lavender Stamp, who presided over the town with a rod of regulation and an iron will to make sure that the mail was always delivered on time. 'Isn't delivering the mail a proper job every day?' she enquired innocently, picking up speed on the subject as Tilly giggled into her scarf.

'Well, if we've got weather, cats don't go out – so there's nothin' in the boxes to collect an' that means there's nothin' to deliver either. If we gets a nice day without weather, then I know I'll be busy 'cause they all go out an' post their letters an' then I can collect 'em up for delivery. Mind you, if the next day is a day when we 'appen to 'ave weather again, I 'ave to wait to deliver, so that means they 'ave to wait.'

'So what about Christmas?' Hettie continued. 'Aren't you really busy at this time of year?'

'Well, we starts the Christmas early you see. If it isn't in the box by the first of December, there's no real chance of it getting there if the weather comes in, and Cornish folk are used to that.'

Hettie decided to give in to Marlon's unshakable logic. It made no difference to her one way or the other, but she inwardly marvelled that Lady Crabstock's summons had ever reached the No. 2 Feline Detective Agency at all if Marlon Brandish had had anything to do with it.

By now, the wildness of the moors had given way to rolling farmland and the occasional small village. The landscape was littered with towering, redundant tin mines standing dark against the melting snow, and, as the daylight began to fade, lamps came on one by one in solitary farmhouses, bringing the countryside to life. As they passed on through the villages, twinkly Christmas lights lit up the windows and kittens swathed in scarves, hats and mittens dragged their toboggans home for tea.

The heat from Lamorna's pasties which had served as a hot-water bottle for the first part of the journey had died down, but the smell of the pastry was becoming unbearable to Hettie; it was some time since they had consumed their full Cornish. 'Shall we stop for a bite to eat?' she suggested, unwrapping the parcel and admiring its contents.

'I'd rather keep the engine running,' said Marlon, swerving into the side of the road as he reached across Tilly for one of the pasties. 'If we stops now we might not get going again, an' we got a few miles yet before we reach Porthladle. You wouldn't want to get stuck out 'ere in the dark.'

Hettie and Tilly agreed, and the three cats contentedly munched their way through Lamorna's parting gift until there was hardly a crumb of evidence left. The rest of the journey was taken up with sharp bends, steep hills and worrying floodwater, and Marlon had to drag himself out of his driver's seat twice to remove branches in the road while Hettie kept her paw on the accelerator, revving it up in case the engine stalled. The thaw had sent torrents of muddy water down from the hills onto the roads, and Marlon strove to negotiate the various hazards as the wind began to pick up, growing ever stronger as they neared the coast and their eventual destination. 'Bad weather comin' in,' he said, almost gleefully. 'I shall be forced to keep myself indoors till this one blows itself out. Shouldn't be surprised if it don't last well into the New Year. Porthladle – she's famous for 'er storms. Folk come from all over to see the waves.'

'Isn't it dangerous?' asked Tilly nervously.

'Only for them that drowns. Waves can pick you up an' throw you into the sea, and there's no chance of bein' saved. Days later you come ashore – naked, skinned, and proper dead.'

Tilly wished she hadn't asked and tried to brighten the conversation. 'I expect Porthladle is lovely in the summer for a seaside holiday, though.'

'Well, that depends. Beaches is too dangerous as the tide comes in when you're not lookin'. An' then there's the rocks.'

Hettie and Tilly waited some time for Marlon

to qualify his statement but, as nothing seemed forthcoming, Hettie did the nudging. 'What about the rocks?'

Marlon rose to the question as he steered them out of a deep trench of water that bubbled across the road. 'Well, take last summer. We'd been battered by the weather all the spring, an' when things calmed down the visitors arrived to enjoy the sun, sand an' sea. They took their picnics down the beach, found themselves a nice spot out of the wind, then crash! All over in seconds.' Marlon paused for dramatic effect, then continued. 'Family of four last time it 'appened, buried from the cliff fall. We found their sandwiches scattered in the sand but it took days for me an' Sooty Perkins to dig 'em out. They sat right under them rocks, they did, an' down they came – loosened by the storms, see.'

Hettie felt that she should ask the obvious question. 'Were there any survivors?'

'No chance! Sooty did a grand job of scrapin' them off the rocks an' we sent what was left of 'em upcountry to their nearest and dearest. We 'ad three lots like that this summer, and then there's the paddle boarders.'

Hettie and Tilly were saved from more of Marlon's morbid tales by the sign that loomed ahead of them, announcing that they had finally arrived in Porthladle. The road into the village was full of twists and turns with the occasional dimly lit cottage, but nothing could have prepared them for the carnival of lights that swung violently across the harbour as they rounded the final bend. Tilly gasped with sheer delight. 'Oh, look! It's so pretty. They've got reindeers in the sky, and fish – and I think that one might be a pasty.'

The light show was certainly impressive, but Hettie was more concerned with the strength of the wind that had hit them full force as they entered the harbour, buffeting Marlon's van to the other side of the road. A tall Christmas tree stood bent and twisted on its moorings at the head of the harbour, threatening to break loose and dance into the sea, and one or two brave cats shrouded in oil skins made slow progress along the pavements, bent double against the blast as they went about their business.

Marlon steered the van past the harbour and up a short but steep hill. Suddenly, without any warning, the vehicle coughed, spluttered and died, and he brought it to what seemed to be a well practised bit of parking outside the Atlantic Inn. The inn sat perched on a high road, overlooking Porthladle's harbour to the right and out across the ocean to the left. Hettie and Tilly waited for Marlon to make some attempt at restarting his van, but instead he opened his door to get out. 'That's as far as we're goin' at the moment,' he said, his words drifting away in the wind. 'Van needs a rest before we try the hill up to Crabstock Manor. Out you get – you may as well stretch your legs an' meet some of the locals.'

Hettie marvelled at Marlon's transparency: clearly the van was going nowhere until he had paid his respects at the bar of the Atlantic, and there was nothing to do but follow him into his own personal port in a storm. The inn was a hubbub of noisy cats drinking, playing various table games, and filling the air with thick smoke from their catnip pipes. Marlon forced his way to the bar while Hettie and Tilly found a seat by the open fire. An elderly cat, much the worse for drink, attempted to serenade Tilly with a rather off-colour sea shanty, but he was soon brought under control by an equally drunk tabby who confiscated his concertina, hurling it onto a table in the corner to interrupt a rather tense game of dominoes. The dominoes flew through the air and showered down onto some of the assembled company as paws were raised, one or two of them landing on unsuspecting chins. Things could have got much worse had it not been for a magnificent black-and-white cat who was serving drinks at the bar; he leapt into the action, grabbing the collars of those keen for a fight and depositing them outside to cool down in the storm.

Marlon managed to make his way across to the fire with three pints of Doom Bar. Setting them down on a table, he proceeded to work his way round the immediate area with some introductions, starting with the cat who had dealt so well with the fallout from the dominoes. 'This 'ere is my good friend Mr Sooty Perkins – a cat that 'as a claw in every pie. 'E runs the An Murdress 'Otel. 'E gardens up at Crabstock. 'E builds things out of wood, an' lends a paw on busy nights in 'ere when 'e's not out fishin'.'

Sooty Perkins bowed low to acknowledge Hettie and Tilly. 'I'm pleased to meet you, an' I 'ope your stay will be a nice one over Christmas. If you're lookin' for somewhere to stay, my 'otel is just along the road. The best view in all of Cornwall if you've come to watch the weather, an' my breakfast griddle is as famous as the great storm of '75.'

Hettie and Tilly instantly liked Sooty Perkins, and felt quite sorry to have to turn down his hotel. 'I'm afraid we're staying at Crabstock Manor,' Hettie explained, 'but if we weren't, we would love to try your griddle.'

Sooty laughed. 'Well, let me just say this – if you 'ave any trouble up at the manor, you get yourselves out of there an' come to me. Odd things is 'appening up there, an' that might not be to your likin'. An' watch out for them Bunns.' He didn't stay long enough to expand on the warning, and Hettie wasn't sure whether he meant the food or the servants, but there was no doubt that they were set on a course to find out.

Marlon continued with his introductions, and Hettie and Tilly nodded to a sea of faces and a host

93

of nicknames: Salty; Scrumpy; Potsy; Dory; Welks; Boy Cockle – who wouldn't see seventy again – and Loveday Whisk, a buxom cat who would share a joke with anyone willing to top up her tumbler with rum. An hour and two more pints of Doom Bar passed before Marlon was finally ready to make his delivery to Crabstock Manor. Hettie and Tilly had only taken small sips from their drinks before passing them on to Boy Cockle while no one was looking. It occurred to Hettie that they would need a clear head for their first meeting with Lady Crabstock-Singe – and she was right.

# CHAPTER TWELVE

Back in Marlon's van, it was no surprise that the vehicle started first time. Refreshed from his drinks, the post-cat forced the van into gear and pulled away from the Atlantic Inn, following the road down the hill and taking the coastal route out of the village. Tilly marvelled at the high seas as the little van was buffeted by the winds, and Hettie stared nervously at the windscreen wipers, which had given up in the face of the storm. There was nothing to be seen in front of them but lashing rain as the little van climbed a steep hill with Marlon wishing it on and crunching the gears until they almost came to a standstill. Suddenly it was over. Marlon flung his door open, and the wind nearly ripped it out of his paw. 'Destination straight ahead!' he shouted as he lurched round to the back of the van to haul their luggage out.

Hettie and Tilly clambered out and took charge of the suitcase and tartan shopper, squinting through the rain for any sign of the manor house. Marlon shut the back doors and returned to his driver's seat, wasting no time in turning the van round and heading back towards the village. Abandoned, soaked to the skin and forlorn in every sense, Hettie and Tilly moved forward as the storm reached new heights. They stumbled blindly ahead, fighting the wind and deafened by the roaring noise of the sea which seemed close enough to engulf them at any moment.

Just when all hope had left them, the edifice of Crabstock Manor rose up ahead like a threatening monster – vast, unwelcoming, and straight out of one of Tilly's Hammer Horror films. The two friends clung to each other and dragged their luggage up a flight of steps to a huge oak door. The door looked impregnable, but Hettie hurled herself at it in an attempt to draw attention to those within. It seemed a very long time before the sound of heavy bolts being drawn across punctuated the howling wind. 'Welcome to Crabstock Manor!' shouted the tall, gaunt, grey cat, dressed from head to toe in livery. 'Please step this way.'

Hettie and Tilly fell over the threshold like a pair of half-drowned rats as their saviour relieved them of suitcase and shopper. 'I am Bunn, 'Er Ladyship's butler, 'andy cat, an' estate manager. I am 'ere to offer you whatever comfort you require during your stay at Crabstock. Am I correct in addressin' Miss 'Ettie Bagshot and her plus one?'

'Hettie!' corrected Hettie, before realising that the aitch in her name was unlikely to be used this side of the Tamar. 'And this is my assistant, Miss Tilly Jenkins.'

'Pleased to make your acquaintance,' said Bunn, closing the door and shutting the storm out. 'If you would care to follow me to the kitchens, I'll leave you in the care of Mrs Bunn, the 'ousekeeper. Leave your luggage 'ere and I'll see that it gets to your rooms.'

There was no real time to take in their surroundings. Hettie remembered later that the entrance hall was vast and barn-like with a grand staircase in the centre, but as they were hurried away dripping across the flagstone floors, all the two friends were aware of was a rabbit warren of cold, damp corridors which eventually led to a large kitchen area at the back of the house.

Seated at a long, well-scrubbed table was a cat of gigantic proportions, deeply engrossed in a newspaper which she read with the aid of a pair of spectacles perched on the end of her flat, snubbed nose. Suddenly aware that she had visitors, she abandoned the newsprint and stood to greet her newcomers. There was hardly any difference in height from a sitting position, but it was her width which dominated the room. 'My dears, come in an' warm yourselves,' she said, wielding a poker at the open fire. 'You must be them dee-tectives from upcountry what 'Er Ladyship 'as ordered.'

Hettie exchanged a look with Tilly and put on her best business smile. 'Yes, that's right. We are from the No. 2 Feline Detective Agency. I'm Hettie Bagshot and this is my assistant, Tilly Jenkins.'

'An' I'm Mrs Bunn. Thaa's my professional name, but you can call me Saffron if you like. 'Er Ladyship says all housekeepers 'as to be Mrs on account of decency, even though Hevva the butler refuses to take me up the church to do a proper job. Says I might limit 'is prospects, whatever they are.'

Hettie and Tilly stood rooted to the spot, forming a puddle from their dripping wet clothes as the housekeeper released a tirade of Hevva Bunn's shortcomings on them, caring little for their immediate comfort. It was Tilly who finally silenced her by entering into a bout of violent sneezing which shook the very foundations of Crabstock Manor. Stifling the final throes with a tea towel, Tilly sat down in her self-made puddle to recover herself, giving Hettie an opportunity to move things on. 'I wonder if we might be shown to our rooms so that we can change into some dry clothes and rest? It really has been quite a long day. Unless Lady Crabstock-Twinge wishes to see us tonight?'

'Singe!' corrected Tilly, scrambling to her feet.

'You're 'avin a laarf if you thinks 'Er Ladyship receives visitors at this time of night! She 'as 'er dinner at seven an' retires to 'er rooms. Locks 'erself in, she does, on account of Christmas!'

'Doesn't she like Christmas?' asked Hettie, noticing that the kitchen held no promise of festive delights.

'She don't mind Christmas, as such. It's Christmas Paws she locks 'er doors against on account of the curse of the Crabstocks. You see it all 'appened a long . . .'

'Thaa's enough of your nonsense, Mrs Bunn, if you don't mind,' said Hevva, lurking in the doorway. 'Your rooms are ready if you would like to follow me.'

Tilly was sorry to be torn away from what promised to be an interesting version of the Christmas Paws story, but the thought of dry pyjamas and a warm bed beckoned and they followed the butler back down the corridor, leaving Saffron Bunn to return to her *Porthladle Gazette*. The rabbit warren seemed less confusing this time. Instead of returning to the front hallway, Hevva took them up a flight of dimly lit stone steps, eventually emerging into a galleried hallway above the main staircase. The gallery was peppered with doors and giant portraits of what Hettie assumed to be the long-dead aristocats of Crabstock.

'I've taken the liberty of putting you in adjoining rooms,' said Hevva, opening one of the doors. 'This 'ere is the blue room an' the one through there is the yellow one. If you'd like to make yourselves comfortable, I'll 'ave Mrs Bunn bring you a tray up for your supper as you've missed your dinner. An' don't take any notice of 'er stories. 'Er tongue runs away with 'er sometimes.' On that slightly warning note, Hevva Bunn left them to explore their new accommodation.

The wood panelling in the blue room was painted a dark muddy brown and was relieved by an equally muddy pink wallpaper above the dado rail. The four-poster bed was draped in velvet curtains which tried desperately to match, but the overall effect was one of faded nobility. Try as they might, Hettie and Tilly could find no trace of blue anywhere, but the saving grace was a small fire in the grate which guttered and twisted as if it was embarrassed to be there at all. Intrigued by what might lie on the other side of the adjoining door, Hettie wasted no time in breaching the threshold of the yellow room, with Tilly following close behind. The same muddy brown panelling gave way to a sage green wallpaper that had never seen yellow in its lifetime; by way of a real contrast, the bed curtains were a dull grey velvet, embellished with black fleur-de-lys in a repeating pattern. The yellow room had no fire in the grate, and a very strong smell of fish.

'I think we'll stick with the blue room,' Hettie said. 'At least it has a fire of sorts and I think we should stay together. I wouldn't trust either of the Bunns not to murder us in our beds, and I can only imagine what tomorrow will bring when we get to meet Lady Eloise Crabstock-Twinge.'

'Singe!' said Tilly automatically, wheeling her shopper through from the yellow room and parking it at the bottom of the four-poster. 'It all seems a bit creepy, and it certainly isn't the stately home Christmas I was hoping for. They haven't put any decorations up, there was nothing lovely being baked in that kitchen, and it's so cold everywhere.'

'Let's stoke this poor old fire up and get into our pyjamas,' suggested Hettie, opening the suitcase. 'If we don't like the look of things in the morning, we'll go and stay at Sooty Perkins' hotel in the village. He seems a reliable sort of cat – almost normal compared to the rest of them.'

The two cats peeled off their wet clothes, discarding them in a heap by the door, and climbed into their winter pyjamas. 'Oh, that's lovely,' said Tilly, hugging herself. 'I didn't think I'd ever be warm and dry again.'

Hettie agreed and returned to the suitcase, delving deep to find the hot-water bottle that Tilly had packed. 'When Saffron Bunn turns up with our supper, I'll ask her to fill this. I bet that bed hasn't been slept in for years. In fact, I bet the last cat to die in it is still in there somewhere.'

Tilly giggled nervously. 'Do you think we should have a closer look?'

The two cats approached the four-poster bed and Hettie bravely pulled the curtains back to reveal nothing out of the ordinary: two pillows; a number of warm blankets; and a slightly faded eiderdown. The bed looked comfortable and Tilly suddenly realised how tired she was. Her arthritic paws were aching from the cold and damp, and she wanted nothing better than to curl up with her hot-water bottle and sleep.

Saffron Bunn put paid to that idea by arriving with their supper. A cursory knock was followed by a kick to the blue-room door, revealing the housekeeper and a tray covered with a rather grubby tea towel. ''Ere's yer supper. Which room will you 'ave it in?'

'We thought we'd share this room as it has the fire,' said Hettie, doing her best not to sound too ungrateful.

'Very sensible, if I may say so,' Saffron replied as she banged the tray down on an old chest by the window. 'No one likes the yellow room – too many of them bad vibrations floatin' about. 'Er Ladyship likes us to keep it locked so nothin' can get to 'er. She's not overkeen on the blue, either, but we 'as to put the visitors somewhere. Not that we 'as many visitors, but these two rooms is the only ones decent on account of 'er low moods.'

Hettie was fascinated by Saffron Bunn's overview of her employer, and thought a little research may help when they came face-to-face with the lady of the manor the next day. 'What sort of low moods does she have?'

'Black ones,' responded Saffron, warming to her subject. 'She don't care for the 'ouse any more. She's lettin' it go. Since 'er sister an' brothers was taken, she just sits waitin' for 'er turn. 'Tis the curse of the Crabstocks, an' she's the laast of 'em.'

Hettie joined Tilly by the fire as Saffron settled herself on the other end of the chest by the window. 'So what exactly is the curse of the Crabstocks?'

'Well, that depends on 'ow you look at it. You see, the Christmas Paws thing comes from way back, but before that there was Pullet Crop an' 'Er Ladyship, Purrditer Crabstock. It was them that started the trouble, really, by taintin' the line. She couldn't keep 'er paws off any of the estate workers. She came as a kitten bride to Crabstock, see – the old Lord was past 'is best an' she looked round for comforts, shall we say. Pullet fancied 'imself above 'is station an' she was partial to a boiled egg, an' the rest is 'istory. Melrose Crabstock was Purrditer an' Pullet Crop's boy, an' it was 'im that done away with Christmas, see? 'E went on to 'ave proper Crabstocks, but 'e wasn't a proper

Crabstock on account of Pullet bein' 'is father.'

Hettie and Tilly were doing their best to keep up, and Hettie decided to ask for a little more clarity. 'That means any Crabstocks after Melrose weren't *real* Crabstocks – so why are they cursed?'

'Ah, well – Melrose married 'is sister when no one was lookin', an' as far as we know she was a real Crabstock, so all 'er kittens was almost full Crabstocks an' Christmas Paws cursed all the Crabstocks as she fell from the cliff just 'ere outside this window. That wasn't outside the window then 'cause there was more cliff, but sea's taken most of it now. You can open your window an' spit in the sea these days, if the mood takes you. Yellow room's even worse – that's 'angin' over the cliff. I don't put too much in there in case it goes altogether. 'Er Ladyship says the sea'll take the manor in time, that's why she's let things go. She says that Christmas Paws will 'ave 'er revenge on the 'ouse when all the Crabstocks 'as gone, an' she is the laast one.'

'And what about the vibrations in the yellow room?' asked Tilly, keen to explore the more bizarre aspects of the story.

'All I can say is keep your doors locked an' try not to . . .'

Once again, Saffron Bunn was interrupted by Hevva, who loomed large in the open doorway of the room carrying two stone hot-water bottles. 'Now then, Mrs Bunn – time you were about your business. No need for all that idle chatter. I expect our visitors want to 'ave their supper an' get to their beds on a night such as this.'

Hettie gratefully took delivery of the bottles and slid them into the bed as the Bunns beat a hasty retreat, banging the door behind them. Tilly responded by turning the large iron keys in the blue-room door, then the one that led to the fated yellow room. Safely locked inside their own small part of Crabstock Manor, the friends dragged the supper tray to the fire and Tilly lifted the tea towel to reveal their first taste of Saffron Bunn's cooking.

Looks are not necessarily everything, but – coupled with an offensive smell and an array of rather poor crockery – Mrs Bunn's idea of supper fell very short of the mark. There were two bowls filled with what might have been grey porridge had it not been for the intense aroma of kippers that the mixture exuded. Next to the bowls was a plate of plain dry biscuits, overbaked and burnt at the edges. It was a rare thing for Hettie to refuse a meal; no matter what was put before her, she could usually summon up some interest, but as she watched Tilly shrink away from the vile concoction, her mind was made up that they would go to bed hungry rather than explore the horrors of the supper tray. As if covering an unsightly corpse, Hettie threw the tea towel over the tray and returned it to the chest by the window.

Tired and now very hungry, the cats warmed their paws on the dwindling fire and clambered into the four-poster where the hot-water bottles had made some attempt at taking the chill away. Tilly pulled the covers over her head and wriggled, making a warm nest for herself; Hettie lay awake, staring at the canopy above her and trying to decide whether to close the bed curtains or not. Would it be more frightening not to see something approach the bed? Or would it be more reassuring to block the rest of the room out? She was still considering this when Tilly sat bolt upright. 'The Butters!' she exclaimed, loud enough to wake the long dead of Crabstock. 'We've still got food in my shopper!' She leapt out of bed, grabbed the shopper, and dragged it up onto the four-poster.

Hettie responded by helping to unpack the greaseproof parcels. Some were slightly worse for wear thanks to Evergreen Flinch, but on closer inspection the food still looked edible and enticing. 'The iced fancies have suffered a bit,' said Hettie, sharing the bits out onto the eiderdown, 'but the cheese rolls and scones are all in one piece, and we've plenty of fiery ginger beer.'

'And look,' said Tilly, unwrapping another parcel. 'I've found a couple of Betty's egg and bacon tarts.' She sniffed each one, deemed them still good, and added them to the growing pile of treats from home.

An hour later, the friends fell into a deep sleep surrounded by crumbs and greaseproof paper, undisturbed by the waves that crashed at their window as the storm gradually blew itself out. But the house was watchful of its visitors, and uneasy about giving up its secrets to strangers.

# CHAPTER THIRTEEN

Hettie and Tilly awoke to the sound of screaming gulls. Tilly padded across the floor to the window and pulled the thick velvet curtains open. The room flooded instantly with light and the view before her was breathtaking. Saffron hadn't been joking about their proximity to the sea: Tilly stared out at a vast expanse of water, so calm that it could as credibly have been a lake as the violent, churning sea of the night before. The gulls wheeled overhead, rising and falling on a gentle wind, and the sun shot a silver path across the sea making everything sparkle. 'Oh come and look at this,' Tilly said, looking back at Hettie who was disentangling herself from the bedclothes. 'We really are on the edge of the cliff.'

Hettie stretched and rubbed her eyes. The extreme

sunlight that Tilly had let into the room was quite a shock, but nothing compared to the shock of gazing down at the tiny amount of rock which appeared to stand between Crabstock Manor and the Atlantic Ocean. 'Well, if Lady Crabstock survives the curse of Christmas Paws, she'll be looking for a new house when her rooms start falling into the sea. Sooty Perkins could cash in big time by renting her his best en suite with views. There's one thing we need to do before anything else this morning, though – open that window.'

Tilly struggled with the catch and the window finally gave way, filling the room with salty air. Hettie picked up the bowls from their untouched supper and spooned the vile, grey, congealed mixture out of the window, where it gradually slid down the rock face and eventually into the sea. A gull swooped and hovered but shrank back with a deafening cry, confirming that there would be no takers for Saffron Bunn's concoction. Tilly broke up the biscuits from the tray and threw them out of the window as well; this time the gulls were keen, and several swooped low to retrieve some of the pieces in mid-air while others fought for scraps on the surface of the water. 'I suppose we'd better get dressed and face Her Ladyship,' said Hettie. 'The sooner we get to the bottom of this Cornish nonsense, the sooner we can go home for our own Christmas. I don't fancy celebrating it at Crabstock Manor.'

Tilly had to agree that her idea of a Cornish Christmas didn't include grey porridge and creepy servants, in spite of the sea view. 'It seems to me that someone is playing tricks,' she said, selecting one of her better cardigans from the suitcase. 'If Lady Crabstock-Singe is frightened of being murdered by a ghost, that all sounds a bit far-fetched. What if someone is *making* her believe it? All we'd have to do is find out who that cat is and it's case solved. And it's only the 22nd of December, so we still have a chance of getting home in time for Christmas.'

Hettie had to admire the straightforward way that Tilly approached their forays into detection. They had had some laudable successes since starting the agency, most of them involving acts of greed, stupidity or sheer evil, but the case they were about to involve themselves in had nothing tangible about it at all. It was the stuff of legend, and that could prove a much harder nut to crack. 'I think we'll have a much better idea of what's going on after we've spoken to Her Ladyship,' she said, 'and Mrs Bunn seems happy to let her tongue run away with her, so we may learn more from her as long as Mr Bunn stays out of the way. He doesn't seem too happy about Saffron spending time with us.'

Hettie chose her best business slacks and a striped jumper for their meeting. After a cursory tidy round, they gathered up their wet clothes from the night before and ventured out onto the main staircase, locking the door behind them. The Crabstocks gazed down from their portraits, their eyes following the intruders as they descended into the hall below. Unlike at Jam Makers Inn, there was no enticing aroma of breakfast, just a cold, damp, musty smell, as if the sea had already taken up residency and just popped out for the morning.

Hettie and Tilly stood at the bottom of the great staircase, listening for any sign of life. Tilly counted eight doors and three corridors leading off from the hallway, and they were just deciding which to try when footsteps approached from one of the corridors. Saffron Bunn emerged in mop cap and not-so-clean apron with a feather duster in her paw. 'Ah, you're up then,' she said as she gave the bottom of the staircase a cursory flick. 'You've missed your breakfast. 'Er Ladyship 'as 'ers at ten minutes past six an' we all 'as to do the same. She can't abide cookin' smells after seven. Do you want them clothes dryin'?'

Hettie placed their damp things in the housekeeper's arms. 'Thank you,' she said. 'That would be very kind of you, as we haven't brought another coat with us.'

'Well, I'll do my best. There's weather comin' in tomorrow, so you'll need your coats by then.'

Hettie offered her best smile as a sweetener and pushed on with the job in hand. 'We would like to speak with Lady Crabstock-Hinge this morning. Do you think that will be possible?'

'Singe!' whispered Tilly.

Saffron put her head on one side as if in deep thought. 'Well, she don't see anyone before she's 'ad 'er lunch, but I could send Hevva to ask 'er if she's at 'ome to visitors.'

'Thank you, that would be very helpful,' Hettie said, beginning to find the housekeeper's attitude a little annoying. 'She did send for us, after all, and we have come a very long way.'

'Well, Cornwall *is* a long way – thaa's why most cats come 'ere in the first place. Upcountry's a long way for us to go, but we don't bother much 'cause we're 'appy where we are.'

Hettie's patience was wearing thin and the fact that she had had no breakfast didn't help. 'If you could arrange for us to see Her Ladyship, we can get on with our work.'

'I'll go an' find Hevva dreckly, but I doubt she'll see you till she's 'ad 'er lunch.'

Saffron Bunn disappeared down the corridor she'd emerged from, leaving Hettie and Tilly to kick their heels. Ten minutes passed before more footsteps were heard and this time they belonged to Hevva, no longer dressed in his butler's outfit but sporting tweed breeches and a shooting jacket, and looking every bit the estate manager. ''Er Ladyship will see you at 'arf

112

past two. She's not comin' out of 'er rooms today, but will receive you there. I suggest you take yourselves off for a walk as you've got three 'ours to wait.' He turned on his heel and was gone before Hettie could argue.

'They don't seem very friendly, do they?' observed Tilly, buttoning up her cardigan.

'No, they don't. Come on – let's go and find some food. I wonder how far the village is? It was hard to tell in the storm last night.'

Hettie slid the bolts back on the old front door and tugged it open. It felt strange to be out in the air after the brooding imprisonment of Crabstock Manor, as if the world had somehow regained its perspective. The sun was surprisingly warm on their faces and the gentle sound of the sea was more reassuring than frightening. They set off at a good pace down the long driveway, not caring to look back, and soon reached the main road. In the distance, they could see the first clutch of cottages that marked the boundary to the village.

The road ran alongside the sea, and Tilly marvelled at the sandy beach peppered with giant standing stones that appeared and disappeared as the waves came and went. The tide was coming in and the ever-present gulls waited near the shore for rich pickings as the current brought the fish closer to the land. There were several small fishing boats

113

out in the bay, their sailors busy with their nets, and a cavalcade of gulls waited hopefully for any catch that might be discarded. Everywhere sparkled, and the wide open sky set against the line of the sea gave a feeling of real possibility to the day.

They passed the first few cottages, where a cat was leaning on a broom and holding court to a clutch of unsuspecting hikers, all done up in their walking boots and trying desperately to get away from the tirade of village nonsense. Hettie and Tilly gave them a wide berth and continued down the coastal road towards a clock tower which looked out to sea. They rounded the corner, and there before them was Porthladle harbour and the centre of the village.

The harbourside was peppered with an assortment of shops and cafes, and Hettie was relieved to see that there would be no shortage of possibilities for breakfast. Tilly stared in delight at the array of brightly painted boats, bobbing up and down as the incoming tide lifted them from their bed of mud. 'Look,' she said, dragging Hettie over to the harbour wall. 'There's Sooty Perkins. He's unloading his boat.'

The giant black-and-white cat waved in their direction and beckoned them over to the slipway where he'd been piling up crates of fish. He looked every bit the genuine fishercat, swathed in a bright yellow mac and sou'wester and sporting a wonderful pair of waders. 'Good morning, my dears,' he said, reaching deep into one of his pockets for his pipe. 'I see you've survived your first night up at Crabstock.' Hettie laughed off his comment but Sooty continued. 'Not an 'appy place these days. It seems them Bunns run the manor since 'Er Ladyship took to 'er rooms. I used to look after 'er gardens – she loved 'er flowers – and she was always seen about the village, 'ad a nice word with every cat she met. She'd come down to turn the Christmas lights on for us, but not this year. She's not been seen for weeks now – not since the light procession, really, an' that was the back end of September.' Sooty paused to light his pipe, sending a billow of sweet tobacco smoke out to sea before returning to his subject. 'This Christmas Paws thing 'as really got to 'er. She just 'ides away in that damp old place, waitin' for something bad to 'appen. It's no way for a lady like 'er to live, an' them Bunns don't do much to cheer 'er up. They're out for themselves, an' letting the manor and them gardens go to wrack an' ruin.'

Hettie was fascinated by Sooty's view of Crabstock Manor and its occupants, and had to agree that the Bunns were far from ideal housekeepers. 'If Lady Crabstock-Hinge is so frightened of a servant cat's ghost, why doesn't she sell up and buy a house in the village?'

Sooty Perkins looked thoughtful for a moment,

searching for the right words as Tilly clambered up onto his fish boxes to escape the attention of a very large crab which was making a bid for freedom from one of his pots. 'The thing about 'Er Ladyship is duty,' he said eventually. 'She's big on that sort of thing. She always used to say that as long as you do your duty, your day will 'ave been worthwhile. 'Er family 'as been up at the manor for 'undreds of years, and as she's the last of 'em, she 'as to see it through. Fact is, she's given up on 'erself *and* the manor.'

'So if she's given up, why do you think she's asked for our help?' Hettie asked as the crab made a pincer movement towards her business slacks.

'That I can't say. But I *can* invite you up to my 'otel for a spot of something off my griddle. You look 'arf starved. Give me a minute an' I'll take you up there.'

Sooty selected half a dozen plump mackerel from his catch and the three cats made their way around the harbour and up a steep hill to the An Murdress Hotel, which stood proud and welcoming at the top of the village. The door was open and there were suitcases piled high in a small reception area, where a family of cats was waiting to check in for the Christmas holidays. Sooty shed his fishing outfit at the door and bounded over the reception desk to engage with his newly arrived guests, with whom he seemed very familiar. 'I've put you in number one this year, an' the kittens can share number six as I've got the bunks in there.' The kittens squealed with excitement at the thought of bunk beds, and their parents were equally delighted by the prospect of the room with the finest views down to the harbour and back out to sea.

Sooty dealt quickly and efficiently with the new arrivals, then settled Hettie and Tilly in the small but cheery hotel bar before heading towards the kitchen, armed with his mackerel. The bar was a miniature version of the Atlantic Inn, with low slung beams, polished tables and a fascinating selection of seafaring art on the walls. There were galleons, schooners, tall ships of every kind, and small sailing boats presented in oils and watercolour, and the display left the hotel's clientele in no doubt of the proprietor's enthusiasm for anything that would float. 'It's much nicer here,' said Tilly, admiring the Christmas tree that had been placed in the window. 'There's no sign of Christmas up at Crabstock Manor, and they're all so miserable.'

'I know what you mean.' Hettie sniffed the air as the first sign of cooked fish reached her nostrils. 'And we haven't even met Lady Crabstock-Hinge yet. I bet she'll turn out to be a bundle of festive laughs.'

'Singe!' corrected Tilly impatiently. 'You must get her name right. It seems to me that there's little enough we can do to save her anyway. If Sooty's right, she's given up the ghost.'

Hettie and Tilly giggled at the unintended reference to Christmas Paws, and Sooty Perkins bustled through from his kitchen with two large plates of sizzling mackerel. 'There you are – get your teeth into these little beauties. They don't come much fresher than that – from sea to griddle, an' nothing in between. I'll 'ave to leave you to it, as I promised 'em an 'our up the Atlantic behind the bar, but you can drop in 'ere anytime you like if Crabstock gets too much for you. Dinner's at six most days, an' me griddle's always on if I'm in. Christmas dinner's up the Atlantic this year, so if you're stayin' on you can join the rest of us there.'

Hettie scrambled some coins together to pay for the fish, but Sooty waved the money away and was gone before she could thank him. The mackerel was cooked to perfection and tasted very good indeed, and the friends chewed and licked their way through the meal until only a pile of glistening white bones was left. Satisfied, they sat back in the small bar, taking time to give their faces and whiskers a good clean ahead of their meeting with Eloise Crabstock-Singe.

By the time they left the An Murdress Hotel, the wind had picked up and the serenity of the morning was gradually being eroded by a dark and moody band of cloud coming in from the sea. The waves were significantly more aggressive on the shoreline, and a salty squall had put paid to any hope of sun for the rest of the day. Tilly pulled her cardigan closer to her as they made their way back into the heart of the village, hoping to stock up on some essentials before returning to Crabstock. 'I think we'd better get something in for our supper,' said Hettie, making a beeline for the bakery on the harbour front. 'Just look at the size of those pasties in the window! I doubt that Saffron Bunn could create anything as substantial as those, and if she could, God knows what we'd find inside them. With a cook like her, no wonder Her Ladyship has lost the will to live.'

Tilly giggled as they pushed open the door to the shop, where they were greeted by a short and very round white-faced cat who could easily have been the Cornish branch of the Butter family. 'Now my 'ansomes – what can I get you?'

Hettie pointed her paw in the direction of a tray of freshly baked pasties. 'Two of those would be lovely, please.'

'Ah, but which of those will it be? You 'as a choice, see.' The cat proceeded to give a guided tour of her selection. 'There's skirt or chuck steak in large or larger; short crust or flaky; with or without turnip, more carrot or less potato – an' a cheese one for them that knows no better.'

Hettie knew that a decision had to be made as another cat had come into the bakery and was breathing Doom Bar fumes all over the counter. She turned round, not at all surprised to see the portly red uniform of Marlon Brandish swaying in the doorway. 'I think we'll have two of the larger chuck

119

steak, please – and do you have any cream cakes left?'

'We 'as puffs, splits, slices and 'orns.'

Hettie checked with Tilly who'd retreated to the bread corner to avoid Marlon, and by mutual consent two cream horns were added to their purchase, along with a large carton of milk that Tilly had wrestled from the shop's fridge.

With a rusty clunk, the clock tower announced that it was two o'clock, and Hettie and Tilly made their way back to Crabstock Manor and their audience with Lady Eloise Crabstock-Singe, content in the knowledge that whatever Saffron Bunn dished up for supper, they now had a very edible alternative.

# CHAPTER FOURTEEN

The manor had reverted to its dark, brooding status as they made their way up the drive. The earlier sun that had lifted their spirits was nowhere to be seen, and its absence served to emphasise the desolate nature of the house and its occupants. Staring up at the fortress door, Hettie doubted if the crumbling walls had ever felt joy or optimism. She raised her paw to knock but the door was flung open before she'd completed the task. They were greeted – if that was the word – by Hevva Bunn, who pushed past them and headed off down the driveway.

Hettie and Tilly chose the grand staircase route to their room. There was no sign of Saffron Bunn or her duster, and according to the tall grandfather clock on the first-floor landing, there was still a quarter of an hour to go before their meeting with the lady of the house. Their room was untouched and the bedclothes were just as they had left them, complete with greaseproof wrappers from their midnight feast. Clearly the housekeeper didn't subscribe to any form of room service, but it was a relief to Hettie that their personal space had not been invaded.

Tilly scooted round the room, gathering up an assortment of clothes and putting them away in the suitcase, while Hettie stuffed the detritus of their meal into the tartan shopper and made a rather pathetic attempt at tidying the bed. They were almost shipshape when, after a cursory knock, Saffron Bunn barged her way into the room. ''Er Ladyship will see you now if you'd like to follow me, and I should tell you she's not in the best of moods. 'Er rash is back, so she's 'ad to cover 'erself in ointment to stop the scratchin'.'

They followed the housekeeper along the landing, past the giant staircase and through a door which opened out into a whole new section of the manor – much grander in a faded sort of way, although the decor was as dull and depressing as the rest of the house. Saffron brought the company to a halt at one of the doors and knocked, this time waiting for a command to enter. A muffled voice came from within, and Saffron led the party into the room.

Hettie and Tilly could never have prepared themselves for what confronted them. The room was huge and must have stretched the full length of the house from sea view to driveway. The furniture was ornate, fussy and faded; a clutch of comfortable chairs gathered round a small low table in the bay window overlooking the sea, while the other end of the room had a rather grand dining table complete with candelabra and a silver place setting for two. But it was the middle of the room that made the two cats stare in horror.

The bed that took centre stage was a giant four-poster, painted in gold and silver and swathed in thick lace curtains. It took a few seconds and a sudden movement from within the drapes for them to realise that it was actually occupied, and they would describe the scene later as a giant mosquito net housing a huge harvest spider. 'Miss 'Ettie Bagshot and assistant, Your Ladyship,' boomed Saffron as she squatted in a rather ungainly curtsey. A paw waved a dismissal from behind her nets and Saffron beat a hasty retreat, leaving Hettie and Tilly to face the music.

'I must apologise for my current incapacity,' said a voice from behind the bed curtain. 'I find myself struck down at present with a reoccurring complaint which means I must keep myself from the daylight.'

Hettie stared into the mesh of netting, trying to discern Lady Crabstock-Singe's features, but could only make out a thin, sinewy form wearing a white mask of thick ointment which gave no indication of character. 'It's Miss bloody Havisham!' she said, under her breath but loud enough for Tilly to hear and have to stifle a giggle. 'How may we be of service to you, Your Ladyship?' she continued, addressing the bed nets and trying to move things along. 'I believe you have concerns regarding your own safety?'

'Ah well, I fear I may 'ave engaged you for nothing,' came the reply. 'You see, the ghost of Christmas Paws seems to 'ave gone on 'er way. She 'asn't been seen or noticed in days, an' I think I might 'ave overreacted on account of my family history. I am so sorry to 'ave put you to any trouble, but my estate manager will pay you for any inconvenience and will arrange your return journey from Penzance now that they've cleared the snow from the line.'

Hettie was seething, and even Tilly – who was famous for her mild manners – stifled a growl of anger in her throat. Neither wanted to be dismissed so easily, and as a helpful wave crashed against Her Ladyship's bay window, Hettie moved in closer to the bed. 'Forgive me for having to point this out to Your Ladyship, but my assistant and myself have endured the most difficult of conditions to present ourselves to you at this time of year. We have forfeited our own Christmas, been stranded in the middle of Bodkin Moor, nearly died in a mineshaft, put up with snow, frost and floods, and into the bargain have received very little food or comfort since our arrival at Crabstock Manor. If it is your intention to send us home with a few expenses in our pockets, then you are not the Lady that the folk of Porthladle speak so warmly about.'

Tilly held her breath and waited for the explosion that would surely come from behind the bed curtains, but Lady Eloise Crabstock-Singe's only response was to ring a small hand bell to summon Saffron Bunn, who had clearly been listening on the other side of the door. 'Mrs Bunn, kindly see my guests back to their quarters and send Bunn to me on his return from the village.'

Hettie and Tilly were roughly ushered from the room by the housekeeper, leaving them in no doubt that their audience with Lady Crabstock-Singe was well and truly over. Back in their room, Hettie paced the floor while Tilly searched for anything that would burn in the fireplace and bring some heat to the cold, damp air. A storm was now raging outside their window and the waves thundered against the house from below. It was clear that they would be going nowhere until the weather had died down, and there was nothing to be done but grin and bear it. 'There's more than a smell of fish about this case,' observed Hettie, eyeing up the bakery bag that contained the pasties. 'Why has Her Ladyship had such a change of heart? The note she sent us sounded desperate, so what's changed in a matter of days?'

'Perhaps she just feels a bit silly,' suggested Tilly

as she screwed up balls of greaseproof paper to lay a foundation to the fire. 'Maybe she sent the letter and then thought better of it, but it was too late to stop us.'

'Or maybe she thinks she can treat everyone like servants without any thought for the consequences. These bloody aristocats live in a different world to the rest of us. Look how they treated Christmas Paws – setting a pack of dogs on her and driving her off the cliff. No wonder she came back to haunt them.'

'Well, if she's stopped upsetting Lady Crabstock perhaps she'd like to magic some sticks and coal for this fire.' Tilly put another cardigan on over the one she was already wearing. 'It's starting to get really cold in here, and it would be nice if she could get us a TV, too. We're missing all the Christmas films, and the *Top Cat* Christmas special is on tomorrow.'

Hettie crossed to the window and stared out to sea. The storm had lifted its game and was battering the foundations of the house; there was a constant, deafening howl of wind now, and with the daylight fading and the prospect of a cold and miserable night ahead, she realised that something had to be done. 'Come on,' she said. 'We're not prisoners in some medieval time capsule. If we have to stay here another night, we may as well be comfortable. Let's ruffle some feathers in the servants' quarters.'

The two cats left the blue room, locking the door

behind them, and made their way down the grand staircase in hopes of choosing the right corridor to the Bunns' kitchen. Having stumbled into a broom cupboard, a still room, and a neglected dairy, they finally located the kitchen at the end of a long, dark hallway, but what greeted them was far from the austere atmosphere of their last visit. They heard the music first, and stood in the open doorway to take in the scene before them. The kitchen fire was blazing up the chimney; a stew pot of sorts swung on a hook over the flames; and Saffron Bunn was rolling out pastry at the kitchen table, singing along to a festive selection of tunes which boomed out from a transistor radio. Hevva sat in a tin bath in front of the fire, with steam rising from the soapy water as he stretched out in the suds, looking like a cat without a care in the world.

Hettie's anger rose and her hackles stood on end. The contrast between their room and the joyful comfort of the Bunns' kitchen was too much for her, and she strode into the room to make her presence felt with Tilly close behind her. 'In case you hadn't noticed,' she began, 'we are guests of Her Ladyship and would like to be treated as such. Our room is freezing, we've been offered nothing in the way of food and drink, and thanks to the weather, we are forced to stay here another night. What are you going to do about it?'

'Nothing!' came the reply from the tin bath. ''Er Ladyship 'as made it clear that she don't need you pokin' around in 'er business, an' we gets paid by 'er, not you. If you wants waitin' on, you can get your own servants. You're lucky to 'ave a room on a night such as this, and if the weather clears I'll be takin' you to your train in the mornin'.'

Saffron continued to roll out her pastry as if there were no conversation taking place, but Hettie decided to stand her ground. 'We are still officially working for Lady Crabstock-Hinge.'

'Singe,' whispered Tilly, giving Hettie a nudge in the back.

'Whilst we are staying here,' Hettie continued, 'we are engaged on an hourly rate whether we are detecting or not, and under those circumstances I insist that we see Lady Crabstock-Hin . . . er . . . Twinge immediately so that I may put in a formal complaint about your behaviour.'

Hevva Bunn threw back his head and laughed, sending water and soap suds splashing across the flagstone floor. 'You cats from upcountry think you're so special, demanding comforts for no work, and if you think 'Er Ladyship will be interested in anythin' you've got to say, then you're more stupid than most of your kind. You've 'ad your chat with 'er, she's told you you're not needed – that's an end to it, so get yourselves back to your room and if you're very lucky Mrs Bunn might bring you some supper. An' don't forget to lock your door – we wouldn't want anything

128

to 'appen to you in the night, would we, Mrs Bunn?'

It was Saffron's turn to give a loud, raucous laugh, wiping tears of merriment away with her flour-covered paws. Hettie's eyes were stinging with tears of anger as she turned abruptly and left the kitchen without another word. Tilly followed close behind and the Bunns' laughter rang out down the corridor after them.

# CHAPTER FIFTEEN

Back in their room Hettie slumped down on the bed while Tilly lit the scraps of greaseproof paper in the grate, adding a few bits of broken festive biscuit which she'd found in the bottom of her shopper. Surprisingly, the biscuits gave a good amount of heat but it was all very short-lived and the concoction in the fireplace was reduced to black ash within minutes.

'At least we have a lovely supper,' Tilly said, trying to brighten Hettie's mood. 'Looks like another bed picnic – and there are cream horns for pudding.'

'That's a very small light at the end of a bloody dark tunnel,' said Hettie ungraciously. 'I don't see why the Bunns should get away with it, and there's something not quite right about this set-up. I keep thinking about Sooty Perkins' warning – he obviously doesn't trust the Bunns, and why has Her Ladyship taken to her rooms and become so reclusive if she isn't afraid of Christmas Paws any more? Why isn't she down in the village more often if she's so friendly with the natives?'

'She didn't seem very nice to me,' said Tilly, wrapping the eiderdown around her shoulders and sitting next to Hettie on the bed.

They sat for some time as the room gradually dimmed and the light disappeared from the window. The storm continued to rage, and Hettie shivered as she got up to close the curtains, lighting a small oil lamp which she placed by their bed. 'Give me the waiting room at Bodkin Station any day,' she said, digging deep to recover her sense of humour. 'Compared to this it's positively five star.'

Tilly obliged with a small giggle and was suddenly transported in her mind back to their jolly evening at Jam Makers Inn. 'What I don't understand is how someone as horrid as Hevva Bunn could possibly be brother to a cat as lovely as Lamorna Tweek.'

'I can certainly understand why she wanted to get away from here. She's got more hospitality in a single claw than the Bunns will ever aspire to, and speaking of hospitality, we could make a run for it.'

'What do you mean?' Tilly sat up straight and looked at Hettie.

'I mean we could get packed up and fight our way through the storm to the village. Sooty Perkins will put us up, even if we have to sleep in his bar.'

Tilly clapped her paws together with delight at the prospect of escaping from Crabstock Manor and the Bunns. 'Ooh, yes. Let's get our coats.'

They sprang from the bed, throwing any stray clothes into the suitcase before Hettie snapped the catches shut. Tilly loaded her tartan shopper with the pasties, cream horns and the carton of milk. They climbed into their wellingtons and both suddenly came to a standstill in the middle of the room. Tilly was the first to speak. 'They've got our coats! Saffron took them away this morning. We can't go out in this weather without them, and if we do leave we'll never get them back.'

Deflated, Hettie sat down on the suitcase. 'Maybe we should just sit it out until they've gone to bed, then we can find our coats and get out of here. With a bit of luck, the storm will have blown itself out by then. Let's have the pasties to cheer ourselves up. Looking on the bright side, we might even be home by Christmas.'

Tilly dived into the shopper to retrieve the pasties as Saffron Bunn burst into the room and banged a tray down on the chest by the window. As before, a filthy tea towel covered the offering and this time the housekeeper left them to it without a word, slamming the door behind her.

Hettie rose from the suitcase and turned the key in the door to make sure that there would be no

132

more impromptu visits from their hosts, while Tilly stood waiting to reveal the delights of Saffron Bunn's culinary artistry. With much ceremony, she whisked the tea towel away from the tray to reveal two wooden bowls of congealed stew. The fat glistened on the surface, daring the most adventurous explorer to delve beneath, and to accompany the putrid concoction, the 'cook' had chosen two thick-cut slices of dry bread, each sporting a healthy dose of blue mould.

'Well, she's certainly surpassed herself this time,' said Hettie, 'but those wooden bowls are just what we need.'

Tilly watched with interest as Hettie turned the bowls upside down on the tray, allowing the stew to run out over the mouldy bread. She carried the bowls to the fireplace, and – with the help of some of the congealed fat – set light to one of them in the grate. Within minutes, the bowl sizzled and spat, sending cheery flames up the chimney and a modicum of heat into the room. Tilly grabbed the pasties and the milk from the shopper as Hettie dragged the eiderdown off the bed, and they sat in a cocoon by the small fire munching their way through the pasties as if they didn't have a care in the world.

The first wooden bowl lasted for some time. Encouraged by her success, Hettie was brave enough to introduce the stew to the flames, which gave out a remarkable intensity of heat, and the final wooden bowl was timed to coincide with the demolition of the cream horns. They were a particular favourite of Tilly's and she had her own unique way of eating one: first the cream was sucked out of the horn along with any jam she encountered along the way; then the horn itself was systematically nibbled down until only the pointy end – as she liked to call it – was left. Hettie watched with admiration as Tilly posted the final piece into her mouth and proceeded to devote the next half an hour to cleaning her face and whiskers. Hettie had eaten her own cream horn with very little ceremony, and relaxed in the dwindling light of the final wooden bowl as it turned to ash in the grate.

The warmth of the fire and the comfort of full stomachs lulled the two cats into sleep, until Hettie awoke with a start several hours later. Sitting up, she cautiously looked around to get her bearings. A strange silence hung in the room, and it was moments before she realised that the deafening roar of the storm had ceased. The silence was louder than any wind and she gently shook Tilly awake, needing a companion to share it with. Tilly sneezed and rubbed her eyes, pulling the eiderdown closer to her to fight the cold that had followed the dying of the fire. 'I think we should make a move now,' whispered Hettie as she fetched the oil lamp from beside the bed. 'The storm has died down and if we can find our coats we can get out of here.' She moved to the window and pulled the curtain aside. It was still dark, and all she could see was the slightest hint of light out at sea where the new day was a small possibility.

Tilly struggled to her feet and stumbled into her wellingtons. 'Shall we take the bags down first in case we have to make a run for it? I wouldn't want to leave my shopper in this horrid place.'

'Good idea,' said Hettie, trying not to make a noise as she unlocked the door. 'But hurry up – there's no time to lose.'

Hettie took the suitcase and Tilly followed on with the shopper, taking care not to allow its squeaky wheels to touch the floor. The grand staircase proved to be a perilous journey in the dark; nothing was familiar, and it was very much a case of the blind leading the blind. There was a terrible moment when both Hettie and Tilly thought they had reached the bottom, only to discover that they were two steps away from firm ground. The baronial banister saved them just in time, but the shopper broke free of Tilly's paws and clattered to the bottom of the stairs. The two cats froze, waiting to be discovered, but no one came and the only witnesses to their descent were the all-seeing eyes of the long-dead Crabstocks, staring down from the walls. Wondering how they had got away with it, they left their luggage at the bottom of the stairs and made their way down the corridor to the servants' quarters. The kitchen door was open and the coals from the fire still glowed, giving them a point of light to aim at. They stopped in the doorway and realised they could go no further: Hevva Bunn was snoring in a chair in front of the fire, an empty tankard hanging from one of his paws.

Hettie and Tilly held their breath and circled the room with their eyes, looking for their coats. Suddenly there came a blood-curdling moan from the corner of the kitchen, followed by a pitiful wail which was repeated over and over again. Bunn woke and sat forward in his chair, staring in the direction of the sound. The groaning and wailing continued, accompanied now by the rhythmic clanking of chains, and the butler rose from his chair and crossed the kitchen to the source of the noises. Hettie and Tilly shrank back into the corridor and watched from a safe distance as a bonneted hag emerged from the corner through a door that they hadn't noticed before. It was hard to see her face, as the bonnet was pulled down almost to her nose, but she wore a rough, coarse dress with an apron over the top. By now, the wailing had lapsed into heart-rending sobs which came from behind the door that the hag had appeared from.

Hettie's heart beat violently in her chest, and she feared that Bunn would hear it and give chase. She signalled to Tilly and the two cats backed away from the kitchen door and hurried down the corridor to rejoin their luggage at the foot of the stairs. The sound of the sobbing had gone by the time they reached the grand staircase, and Hettie was in two minds as to whether they should make a run for it or stay to discover what was really going on. Perhaps Lady Crabstock really did need their help, and running out on a client wasn't the best publicity for a detective agency; from what they had just witnessed, there was plenty to investigate.

Hettie grabbed the suitcase and nodded towards the stairs. Tilly took hold of her shopper and they retraced their footsteps back to the blue room, quietly locking the door behind them. 'What in hell's name was all that about?' demanded Hettie, finding her voice. 'Have we just seen the ghost of Christmas Paws? And who was sobbing and wailing? Was it Saffron Bunn, and if it was, why didn't Hevva try to help her? There's some real nasty stuff going on here and we need to get to the bottom of it.'

Tilly agreed but immediately saw a flaw in the plan. 'If we're being put on a train in the morning, we won't get a chance to look into it. We have to leave. Lady Crabstock-Singe doesn't want us here.'

Hettie thought for a moment. 'We could pretend to get on the train and come back here instead. We could stay at Sooty Perkins' hotel and keep our eye on the manor from a safe distance. I also think we should try and have another chat with Her Ladyship if we can.' She looked out of the window. The daylight was filling the sky and the sea was alive with tiny fishing boats out for an early morning catch, riding the small waves left by the storm. 'There's no reason for us not to be up and about. We're all packed, so let's take the cases down and have an early morning stroll into the village as if nothing had happened. Hevva was too busy with the ghost to notice us.'

Looking around the room to check they had left nothing behind, Hettie and Tilly boldly strode down the grand staircase, leaving their luggage by the door. They made their way down the corridor to the kitchen, but there was no sign of the pantomime they had so recently witnessed. The Bunns sat at either end of the kitchen table, spooning in porridge as if their lives depended on it. A large frying pan sizzled on the range, full of bacon and sausages, and there was a mountain of hot buttered toast ready for the eating. 'I'm so sorry to interrupt your breakfast,' said Hettie with as much sarcasm as she could muster, 'but I was wondering if we might trouble you for the coats that you so kindly agreed to dry out for us? We've decided to go for a last look round the village before we leave today and it's a bit chilly at this time of the morning.'

Hevva Bunn lifted his face from the bowl, spitting

the last mouthful back into the dish and picking his teeth with one of his claws before responding. 'Your train's at ten, and you'd better make sure you're on it. Bus to Penzance goes from the 'arbour at quarter past nine, so you may as well get your stuff and clear out now.' He reached into his trouser pocket and pulled out a collection of notes and coins, throwing them onto the floor at Hettie's feet. ''Er Ladyship 'as instructed me to pay you off, and that should be plenty for your trouble. You can get your tickets out of it, too.'

'That's so kind of you,' said Hettie as Tilly scrambled for the money, making sure she collected every last penny. 'I would just like to say goodbye to Lady Crabstock before we leave if that's all right with you?'

Hevva Bunn rose from the table and brought his paw down with a thump, toppling the mountain of toast and making Saffron spit her tea across the table. 'She's not seein' anyone today, especially not you. She didn't like your tone an' she's not used to being spoken to in such a fashion, so you can get yourselves gone.' Saffron, responding to a nod from Hevva, pushed past Tilly and Hettie and retrieved their coats from a cupboard in the corridor. With a grunt, she pushed the coats at Hettie and made for the range, where she began to pile two plates high with the fried breakfast.

'Oh, how nice of you to offer us such a feast,' Hettie

said, clutching the still-damp coats to her. 'Sadly we couldn't manage another thing after your lovely stew last night. It was so delicious that we ate the bowls as well.' Pleased with their parting shot, the two cats positively chirruped their way back into the hall and out into the early morning sunshine, finally free of the suffocating constraints of Crabstock Manor – at least for now.

# CHAPTER SIXTEEN

The driveway of the house seemed much longer with the added burden of a heavy suitcase and the shopper, which Tilly had to carry as the wheels kept getting stuck in the mud from yesterday's storm. But at least they were walking away from the manor, and that in itself made them joyful enough to give Marlon Brandish a wave as he passed them on the road in his van. It was hard to tell that he had responded by applying his brakes, as they did take some time to work, but it was eventually clear that he had stopped and was waiting for them to catch up.

'Want a lift into the village?' he asked, brushing a pile of bottles and sandwich wrappers off his passenger seat.

Hettie adopted what she liked to think of as her

most winning smile. 'That would be very kind.'

Marlon threw himself out of the van and took charge of the luggage, tossing it into the back with very little ceremony. 'Not staying long at the manor then?' he said, as Hettie and Tilly squeezed themselves in beside him. 'Not that I blame you – odd things goin' on, an' they say that ghost's back again. No wonder 'Er Ladyship's actin' strange.'

'In what way?' Hettie enquired as Marlon coaxed the van through a deep puddle of water.

'Well, I always used to pop in for a chat with 'er. She liked writing 'er letters, an' some days she had six or seven ready for me to take, but I've 'ardly seen 'er these last few months, not till last week, an' that was a rum business.' Hettie waited for Marlon to continue, but instead he brought the van to a standstill and jumped out. They'd reached a clutch of small cottages and the cat who had been holding court with the cliff walkers the day before was again in full sail in her capacity as unofficial tourist information officer. Marlon exchanged a small sack with her for one of a similar size and returned to the van. 'Saves my poor old legs, she does – collects up the letters from all them cottages as she's in an' out of 'em all the day long, then I gives 'er the letters for delivery an' she takes 'em round. Unofficial, like.'

Hettie was still baffled by the Cornish postal system, but was too keen to find out more about Lady

Crabstock and the 'rum business' to worry about it. 'You were telling us about Lady Crabstock and what happened last week?' she coaxed.

'Ah yes. I'd got a parcel for Saffron, see, so I was takin' it round the back to the kitchen door when I saw 'Er Ladyship come to 'er upstairs window. She was wavin' at me like a bit of a mad cat, really, an' I'll tell you this – she was as pale an' wasted as any corpse. I was quite shocked to see 'er like that. Anyway, she opens 'er window an' chucks a letter out. By the time I'd got me paws on it, she'd gone from the window and that was that.'

'And did you notice who the letter was addressed to?' asked Hettie.

'Not straight away. I put it in me pocket and took Saffron 'er parcel, but she wasn't in so I left it on the back doorstep an' went on me way.'

Hettie was getting impatient and it hadn't escaped her notice that Marlon's van had spluttered to a halt outside the Atlantic Inn. She asked the question again. 'So who was Lady Crabstock's letter addressed to?'

'Can't exactly remember now, but it was an odd sort of address. Feline Detection or similar, I think. You'll 'ave to excuse me now as I promised Boy Cockle a game or two of dominoes while I eats me breakfast.' Marlon flung his door open and pulled the suitcase and shopper out of the back of his van. 'There you go! Safe journey 'ome. Bye now.' And with that he

143

disappeared through the front door of the Atlantic, which appeared to be in full swing even though the Porthladle clock tower declared that it was only seven o'clock in the morning.

Hettie and Tilly stood for a moment wondering what to do next. There was at least two hours before the bus to Penzance, and as they didn't now intend to leave the village at all, there seemed very little point in catching it. The idea of a cooked breakfast and a place to lie low for a few hours seemed the obvious plan; in light of Marlon's revelation there was much to discuss. 'Let's go straight to the An Murdress Hotel and see if we can get a room,' said Hettie, picking the suitcase up. 'I think it's along here somewhere, and we may be in luck with Sooty Perkins' griddle.'

Tilly took hold of her tartan shopper with a new enthusiasm at the thought of another meal from Sooty Perkins, and the two cats had gone only a matter of yards before the welcoming frontage loomed into view. Sooty was in the bay window of his bar as they approached, adding a few more baubles to his tree, and he immediately came out to meet them. 'Are you staying or going with those cases?'

'We'd very much like to stay if you have a room?' said Hettie, as Tilly bumped her shopper into the hotel's reception area.

Sooty sprang behind the desk and picked a bunch of keys off a hook. 'I'll put you in number two – sea and

144

'arbour views, but a slight knockin' from my 'ot-water pipes. For that, you gets a slight reduction. You got twins in there, and it's lovely and warm as it's right above my sitting-room fire.' Sooty's description of the room sounded like manna from heaven after their recent accommodation, and Hettie and Tilly followed him up the stairs to the sheer luxury of one of his best rooms. 'Make yourselves at 'ome. You got an 'our till breakfast, but you got facilities over there for a nice cup of tea and a biscuit or two. Just shout if you need anything.'

He left them to it and Tilly put the kettle on and prepared two mugs. 'These biscuits look lovely,' she said as Hettie kicked off her wellingtons and chose one of the twin beds.

'*Everything* is suddenly lovely.' Hettie looked round, admiring the festive touches to their room. There was a small silver tree on the dressing table, decorated with tiny glass baubles, and red candles in the bedside holders. The room smelt of nutmeg and cloves, which Tilly traced to a pomander over the sink, and the view from the double bay window was all Sooty said it would be. They sat in the window to eat their biscuits and drink their tea, watching as the harbour came to life, and when the aroma of a cooked breakfast began to creep under their door, they couldn't have been more content. There was a difficult job to be done, but not until they had explored the full potential of Sooty Perkins' griddle.

The guests in room number one were leaving for a day out as Tilly and Hettie struggled down to the breakfast room. The two excited kittens were bouncing on the sofa in the reception area as Sooty held court, reeling off a whole list of places to visit. 'You should 'ave a trip out to Goonsilly to see those big dishes pointing to the sky – almost as big as my breakfasts, they are. Then there's the Poldark mines off the telly, an' if you've a mind for giant vegetables you could take yourselves up the Eden Project – Tim Spit runs that, an' 'e's stuck all 'is flowers an' veg in a big old dome so you don't get wet going round. On the way back you could try to find the Lost Gardens of Heligan – not easy, since the locals 'as taken all the signs down 'cause they got fed up with the visitors, but it's worth a look. Story goes that all the cats who were employed as gardeners at Heligan House put down their spades and marched off to the Great War, leaving the gardens to grow wild. Tim Spit come along years later and 'acked 'is way in to put 'em back to their old ways. That's probably a visit for the summer, though, come to think of it.'

Sooty waved his guests on their way and headed for his breakfast room, where Hettie and Tilly had made themselves at home. 'Now then,' he began, 'what can I tempt you with? You look like you're in need of my breakfast platter and two plates.'

Tilly liked the sound of a breakfast platter and

nodded enthusiastically. Hettie – trusting that anything from Sooty's griddle would be substantial and delicious – agreed with his recommendation, too, and within minutes the hotelier returned bearing a giant oval plate loaded with every breakfast item a cat's heart could desire. Tilly was so excited that she felt it her duty to announce each individual item on the platter. 'Bacon, eggs, black pudding, one . . . two . . . three sorts of sausage, chops and . . . oh, I'm not sure what they are.'

She pointed to a collection of golden squares and Sooty came to her rescue. 'That is my special eggy bread. It's a favourite with my guests and they 'ave to order the platter to get it, so you're in luck. Get tucked in and I'll fetch your toast and tea.'

'I'm beginning to like Cornwall,' said Hettie, opening her napkin and tucking it firmly into the neckline of her jumper ready for her first assault on the plate in front of her. 'Maybe we should start a Cornish branch of the No. 2 Feline Detective Agency? I bet there's plenty of mysteries round here to solve.'

Tilly giggled and pitched into the eggy bread, nibbling the corner at first, then wholeheartedly embracing it before moving on to the sausages. Sooty returned with the tea and toast and joined them at the table, bringing his own giant breakfast sandwich with him. 'I'm not pryin' or anything,' he began, 'but I get the feeling that you've 'ad a bit of a rough time up at Crabstock Manor, and if there's anything I can 'elp you with, all you 'ave to do is ask.'

Hettie was thoughtful for a moment as she chewed her bacon, weighing up the situation they found themselves in. The Crabstock case was going to need some local knowledge, but the Bunns were proving to be formidable enemies and no help whatsoever. Sooty, she felt, was a cat they could trust: he had, after all, come to their rescue twice within the last twenty-four hours. Making her mind up, Hettie recounted the case so far with Tilly chipping in on the bits she had forgotten. Sooty listened carefully, saying nothing but nodding sagely at various points as the three cats demolished everything on the breakfast table except the pottery and tablecloth. When Hettie concluded the sorry tale, Sooty's normally optimistic face took on a look of grave concern. Without a word, he piled up the empty plates and took them through to his kitchen.

Hettie and Tilly stared at each other, hoping that they had done the right thing by taking Sooty into their confidence; on his return, they were left in no doubt that he had become their latest unpaid recruit. 'Let's go through to the bar,' he said, wielding a rolled-up piece of paper. 'I've got something to show you.' The three cats settled themselves down and Sooty opened up the roll to reveal a plan of some kind. He stretched the paper out on the table, employing two heavy ashtrays to stop it from rolling up. 'This is an old plan of the manor. It shows where all the rooms are, an' there's one or two secret passageways marked up to 'elp with the smuggling.'

Tilly was quite excited at the prospect of smugglers. 'So do they do that up there as well?'

Sooty laughed. 'No, my dear, not any more. These passageways go back a long way to the days of the tall ships and schooners that got wrecked on the rocks carrying all sorts from the Indies – tea, silk and the best Jamaican rum. Now you can get all that from a day out in Penzance.'

Deflated, Tilly stared round the bar at the old ships that adorned the walls, imagining the days of swashbuckling pirates and recalling one of her favourite books where the loathsome Captain Hook wielded his cutlass. There was a crash from the kitchen and Sooty went to investigate, leaving them to pore over the house plan. It had clearly been drawn up in better days, as there was a grand ballroom, a number of salons, several state rooms, and a whole warren of servants' quarters and cellars. 'Sorry about that,' said Sooty. 'My daily 'elp got a bit too enthusiastic with 'er washin' up. 'Ave you met Loveday Whisk yet? I think she was up at the Atlantic the night you arrived.'

'Is she the one who drinks rum?' asked Tilly.

'Yup, that's 'er. She's made a career of it since she

left the manor. Come to think of it, you should 'ave a chat with 'er when she's finished my rooms. She worked in the kitchens up there when the murders were 'appenin'. She's a good worker as long as you can catch 'er before she starts 'er daily dose, as she calls it. No sense out of 'er after that, although you might 'ave to oil 'er wheels to get 'er talkin', if you know what I mean. Now, let's 'ave a look at this plan. Where did you say you saw the ghost?'

Hettie located the kitchen and pointed to a door marked in the corner of it. 'It came out of there, I think.'

Sooty studied the kitchen area. 'That door leads down to the old wine cellar. I know that bit quite well 'cause I used to store my lawnmower in there until the sea took the lawn. You can get to it from outside, see, without botherin' anyone from the 'ouse. Sea comes right up to the cellar now, an' you wouldn't want to be down there in bad weather. If my old memory serves me well, that's where they found Wingate – butchered, 'e was, with 'is eyes gouged out.'

'Wingate?' queried Hettie.

'Yes,'Er Ladyship's oldest brother. Thirty-first Lord of Crabstock, to give 'im 'is proper title. Bit of a philanderer, but fair to 'is tenants. I always got on well with 'im. Built 'im a pineapple house 'cause 'e wanted to grow exotics up at the manor. Awful, really – that's where they found little Tamsyn, 'Er Ladyship's younger sister, 'er 'ead caved in an' a bloodied pineapple lying next to 'er. I 'ad orders to pull the thing down after that.'

'Didn't Her Ladyship have two brothers?' asked Hettie, impressed by the creative way in which the departed of Crabstock Manor had departed.

'Ah, you'd be referrin' to Willmott,' said Sooty as another crash came from above, signalling that Loveday Whisk was now about her work in bedroom number one. "E was an evil little sod. No one bothered much when 'e went, pinned to the kitchen table with four nice sharp knives and left to die of 'is wounds. Poor Loveday spent weeks scrubbin' that table, tryin' to get the blood out. They say that's what turned 'er to the drink.'

'That all sounds to me like a vicious killer who has it in for the Crabstocks,' said Hettie. 'Why would anyone even consider that a ghost would be involved when there's obviously a murderer on the loose?'

'That's true enough,' said Sooty. 'But you forget you're now in the land of myths and legends, and the curse of the Crabstocks is an acceptable fact round 'ere. Christmas Paws stands as a beacon to all cats treated badly by their employers, and anyway you say you've seen 'er – round 'ere, seein' is believin'.'

'I've seen 'er,' said a voice from the doorway.

'Ah, Loveday – if you've finished your work, could

151

you spare yourself to 'ave a chat with my friends 'ere about your days up at the manor?'

Loveday Whisk shrank back in the doorway and began licking her paws nervously. 'I can't speak of the manor. My fur will fall out. Tha's only just grown back.'

Sooty stood up. 'Now come on, there's nothing to be afraid of. Come an' sit down with 'Ettie and Tilly – they don't bite. Perhaps a tot or two of your favourite might help?' Loveday came forward and perched herself on the edge of a low stool. Sooty went behind his bar and returned with a bottle of rum and a small tumbler which he placed in front of Loveday. ''Ettie and Tilly are proper detectives from upcountry and they've come to 'elp 'Er Ladyship up at Crabstock. I know you likes 'Er Ladyship and would do anything to 'elp 'er, so now's your chance.'

Loveday nodded and Sooty filled the small tumbler with rum, which she downed in one. 'Right! Now you've got some Cornish courage in you, you tell my friends 'ere about your time up at the manor.' Sooty put the stopper back in the rum and stood it behind the bar. 'You can 'ave another tot after you've finished. I got some paperwork to do, so I'll just be out in reception if you need me.'

Hettie watched as Sooty made himself scarce, then turned to Loveday Whisk, who sat trembling before them. 'Please don't be frightened. We just need to ask a few questions about life up at Crabstock and the cats you worked with. If you like, you're our undercover agent.'

Loveday brightened at Hettie's words. 'Undercover? Does that mean I'm important?' she asked, brushing some dust from the hem of her apron.

'It means you're *very* important, and vital to the case. When did you leave the manor and why?'

Tilly pulled a notepad and pencil from her cardigan pocket, poised to take statements on a page entitled 'THE CRABSTOCK CASE'. She nodded, and Loveday began her story. 'I got out of there soon as I could after Master Willmott. I couldn't take no more of it. Mr Bunn made me scrub till all the blood was gone, an' my paws was bleedin' with the work. I found 'im, see, stretched out 'e was like a chicken waitin' to be stuffed, 'is face all twisted from the pain.'

Hettie was tempted to clarify some of Loveday's remarks but thought better of it; she seemed to be doing well without prompting, and some of the more glaring knots of her story could be unravelled later. Tilly scribbled away, trying to keep pace as Loveday got into her stride. 'Christmas 'ad been seen in the kitchen three nights in a row before I found 'im. Saffron 'ad seen 'er in the pantry an' Mr Bunn said she was 'angin' about the still room. I seen 'er when I was makin' 'Er Ladyship's 'ot chocolate, the night before I found 'im. We did wonder who would be next, as Miss

Eloise was the older one but Willmott was next in line after Lord Wingate, an' 'e went first. Mind you, Lord Wingate didn't 'old with the Christmas Paws curse. 'E called us all together an' said it was nonsense an' we was to get on with our work, then 'e disappeared upcountry for a bit. Anyway, Christmas 'ad taken to clankin' chains an' sobbin' at night, then Mr Bunn found 'im – Lord Wingate, that is – in the wine cellar below the kitchen, 'is 'eart ripped from 'is body, an' 'is eyes dug out an' put on a saucer next to 'is corpse.'

Tilly gulped and Hettie began to regret the breakfast platter, but there was no stopping Loveday now. 'By the next Christmastime we was all 'oldin' our breath. Master Willmott was the new Lord Crabstock, but 'e wasn't next, as it turned out – which was a shame, really, as 'e was nasty to everyone. 'E turned out some of the locals from their cottages on the estate an' made 'em into 'oliday 'omes for the visitors. 'E put all our wages down an' 'e treated 'is sisters like dirt – married Miss Eloise off to Celibate Singe, one of 'is nasty friends from Fowlmouth, and 'e treated 'er terrible. If 'e hadn't choked 'imself on a fish bone, Miss Eloise would 'ave killed 'im 'erself. We was so pleased to see 'er 'ome again, but then poor Miss Tamsyn got battered to death with a pineapple in the fruit 'ouse an' Lord Willmott, as 'e then was, took to 'is rooms with a barrel of brandy. 'E only came out for a refill an' I 'ad to leave 'is food outside 'is door. 'E made the mistake of comin' down to the kitchen on Christmas Eve of all nights, an' that was that – she 'ad 'im with four of our best sharp knives.'

Pleased with her presentation, Loveday eyed up the bottle of rum that Sooty had put behind the bar. 'Did it occur to anyone up at the manor that someone else might have done the murders?' Hettie asked, pleased to get a proper question in at last.

'Why should it? We all knew that was Christmas Paws on account of the Crabstock curse. She won't rest till they've all gone.'

'What about the Bunns?' asked Hettie, trying a different route. 'Did you get on well with them?'

Loveday's eyes flicked to the rum bottle and then back to Hettie. 'Well, Saffron an' me started up there together. They was lookin' to replace Lamorna, who'd taken off with Absalom Tweek, so we both went up for the interview an' Mr Bunn took a fancy to Saffron an' said I could stay as well. Me an' Saff was good friends, an' we 'ad a good larf up there for a bit till the murders – then it all changed.'

'In what way?'

'Well, we was all a bit shook up an' frightened by Christmas. She was no picture to look at, an' you could tell when she was around on account of the smell – fish, that's what it was, an' she left puddles on the floor, puddles an' seaweed, strands an' strands of the stuff. We all tried to get on with the work but Saff 'ad changed. She'd got closer to Mr Bunn, if you know what I mean. She'd gone up in the world, too good to talk to me. I seemed to be doin' most of 'er work in the end. She'd found a good place for 'erself, but not what I'd call 'appy.'

'Why not?' Hettie coaxed.

Loveday considered her next sentence, wondering if she'd already said too much. Tilly – poised with her pencil – beamed at her to show she was among friends, and Loveday decided to answer the question. 'I used to 'ear 'er sobbing in 'er quarters. My little room was next to theirs. Mr Bunn liked 'er to keep 'erself to 'erself, an' if 'e caught 'er gossiping she'd suffer for it. 'E can be violent if roused. I've seen 'im pinch 'er arms till 'er fur fell out. That's why I left – 'e'd become like a cat with too much power an' 'Er Ladyship just let 'im get on with it. My nerves was all I lived on, an' cleaning up after Lord Willmott was the final straw.'

'What about Her Ladyship? Did you get on well with her?'

Loveday smiled for the first time, as if the sun had broken through the clouds. 'She was lovely to us all. She'd come down to the kitchen and pass the time of day, she'd organise day trips up Penzance and give us spendin' money. She always asked after our families, and if anyone was taken bad she'd send flowers from 'er garden and fruit from the fruit 'ouse so they'd get better quicker – before Miss Tamsyn, that is. She loved

Miss Tamsyn, an' took it bad. She tried to put a brave face on it an' go about 'er business, even tried to keep Lord Willmott on the right side of things, but these days I think she's just 'ad enough. Never see 'er in the village any more. It's almost like she's keepin' 'erself a prisoner up there, an' if you've seen Christmas Paws then I reckon 'Er Ladyship's goin' the same way as the rest of the Crabstocks.'

Hettie nodded to Tilly, signalling that the interview was over. They had more than enough to ponder on, and a deep tiredness had suddenly come over her. She realised that neither of them had slept properly since they'd arrived in Porthladle, and a couple of hours of uninterrupted rest just might help to sharpen their wits. Tomorrow was Christmas Eve, and according to the curse it was likely that it would be the day that the last of the Crabstocks would be struck down. Something had to be done, but Hettie was too tired even to consider what that might be.

Sooty, hearing that Loveday's account of her days up at the manor was over, came back into the bar. True to his word, he collected the rum bottle and moved to fill Loveday's tumbler as a reward for her cooperation, but Loveday swiftly moved to cover the glass with her paw. 'That's kind of you, Sooty, but I think I'll go through to the kitchen an' give your cupboards a good turn-out. I feel better than I've done for months, like some cat's lifted a barrel of dabs off me shoulders. I've no need for a drink. In fact, I fancy a nice cup of tea.' Sooty stared in astonishment, a little unsure of what he was hearing. Before heading for the kitchen, Loveday turned to Hettie and Tilly. 'I 'ope you can 'elp 'Er Ladyship. She don't deserve to be taken by Christmas Paws. She's the only good thing about Crabstock Manor. The rest of it is sheer evil.'

# CHAPTER SEVENTEEN

Back in their room, Hettie and Tilly threw off their clothes and clambered into their twin beds. Within seconds, they were both fast asleep. Seemingly dead to the world, it took several polite knocks on their door from Sooty Perkins to rouse them three hours later. Tilly padded across the floor wrapped in a blanket and opened the door to find a lunch tray piled high with fish-finger sandwiches and a mountain of crisps. 'Lovely!' she murmured to herself as she settled the feast onto the table by the window. The next job – waking Hettie – was a little more difficult. It was a task that Tilly had mastered very early in their friendship, but it always proved a delicate operation. She had the fish fingers on her side, though, and slipped one of them out of a sandwich to lay on Hettie's pillow, only an inch away from her nose, then stood back to watch the result. First came a slight vibration of her whiskers; then a bout of twitching nostrils, followed swiftly by one eye opening to let the light in. Satisfied that the fish finger had done the trick, Tilly busied herself making two mugs of tea as Hettie gradually re-entered the world of the living – which was more than could be said for the fish finger.

Sitting up, Hettie cleaned the remaining breadcrumbs from her whiskers and stretched. 'Is it late?' she asked, pulling her jumper on and exchanging the cosy warm bed for a chair in the window, then helping herself to a pawful of crisps.

Tilly brought the mugs of tea over and squinted across to the clock tower. 'Either three o'clock or a quarter past twelve. It's hard to say from here.'

Hettie launched into a fish-finger sandwich, allowing the butter to run unchallenged down her chin and onto her jumper. Tilly took up a sandwich and proceeded to lift the top slice of bread off so that she could cram as many crisps in before replacing the lid. Opening her mouth as wide as it would go, she took a healthy bite and closed her eyes to enjoy the sheer heaven of bread, crisps, butter and fish fingers, eventually washed down with a mug of milky tea. Satisfied, and covered in butter, they cleaned and preened for some time, enjoying the ritual and relaxing for the first time since they'd arrived in Porthladle – but the Crabstock Manor case required an injection of urgency, and both of them knew it.

Hettie pulled off her butter-stained jumper and selected an outfit of clean but slightly crumpled clothes from the suitcase – a pair of business slacks and a bright red polo-neck jumper to keep the cold out. Seeing that Hettie was going for a seasonal look, Tilly chose her festive cardigan in bright red with snow cats on the pockets. It was her best present from last Christmas, and she had worn it well into April before Hettie suggested that she should put it away for a few months. She completed her look with a pair of bright green woolly socks, ready now to face the day and whatever it may throw at them.

Once they were settled in their window seat, Hettie asked Tilly to run through her notes and observations on Loveday Whisk, then sat staring out to sea deep in thought. 'It seems to me that the answer lies with Lady Crabstock-Hinge,' she said eventually, and Tilly had given up trying to correct her. 'We have to ask ourselves what happens when and if she dies? We're told she's the last of her line so who gets the manor? Three of her siblings have been murdered, none of those deaths could ever be described as accidents, and discounting a very convenient family curse, there must

161

be a cat or cats to link all those murders together, so let's jot down some suspects.'

Tilly immediately took up her pad and pencil. Choosing a clean page, she wrote 'SUSPECTS' and underlined it three times, nodding to Hettie when she was ready to begin. 'The Bunns are an obvious favourite, so put both of them down. They had opportunity and access, and they're horrible anyway. Loveday Whisk is an outsider and so is Sooty Perkins; they both worked up at the manor and had the run of the place, but I wouldn't put my money on either of them. Then, of course, there's Lady Crabstock herself. I could understand her wanting to get rid of her brothers, especially Willmott – she can't have taken too kindly to being married off to Celibate Hinge.'

'Singe!'

'But why would she kill her younger sister? It's not like she was in her way,' Hettie continued, oblivious to the interruption. 'And if she did murder them all, why would she ask us to sort it out?'

Tilly added Lady Crabstock to her list and looked up. 'Aren't we missing the most important suspect? You haven't mentioned Christmas Paws yet.'

'To be honest, I was trying to avoid her altogether. If she *is* hanging round the manor with some old grievance, frightening cats now and again, that's one thing – but gouging eyes out and taking up pineapples and kitchen knives to defend her honour from beyond the grave is almost too much to swallow.'

'But we did see her, and she was horrid,' insisted Tilly.

Hettie conceded the point. 'OK, stick her down with the rest of them. Well I never! Take a look at that.'

Tilly followed the direction of Hettie's paw just in time to see Hevva and Saffron Bunn struggling up the coast road under the weight of one of the biggest Christmas trees she'd ever seen. 'Looks like they're celebrating after all. That must have cost a fortune.'

Hettie agreed. 'I dare say Her Ladyship's got a few shillings put by from the family coffers, but she didn't strike me as the big Christmas tree type when we met her.'

'But Loveday said she was nice.'

'Yes, that's one of the many inconsistencies in this case. I really would have liked to have a proper conversation with her. She was obviously out of sorts yesterday, hiding behind all those net curtains. We didn't even get a proper look at her. Maybe I should have been more polite, but coming all this way to be dismissed with only a pocket full of expenses is enough to make a witch spit.'

Tilly giggled at her friend's turn of phrase. She collected up their tea mugs and rinsed them in their sink, while Hettie continued on the theme of Lady Crabstock. 'Most of the cats we've spoken to agree that she hasn't been herself lately. Sooty says she's been reclusive and doesn't come to the village any more; Marlon Brandish has obviously noticed a change in her letter-writing output; and as for chucking letters out of her window – well, that really is an odd thing to do. If she didn't want to leave her room, why didn't one of the Bunns collect it for her?'

'Because she didn't want them to know about her calling us in, I suppose,' said Tilly, having a light-bulb moment.

'Exactly,' Hettie agreed. 'So let's think about the Bunns and where they sit in all of this. We know they appear to be very protective towards Her Ladyship and they certainly seem to call the shots up at the manor. They both believe in the Christmas Paws nonsense, and Saffron seems convinced that the ghost is at the bottom of all the murders. They seem to be allowing the manor to fall down around their ears while they live the high life at Her Ladyship's expense. They're unwelcoming to strangers and even though we were expected they did their damnedest to keep us away from Lady Crabstock for as long as they could. And why all the warnings about locking our door at night? It didn't stop Evergreen Flinch from reorganising our things at Jam Makers Inn; she just came through the wall, so surely a ghost as notorious as Christmas Paws wouldn't be kept back by a locked door? There's something missing from all of this. I get the feeling that now we're supposedly on the train from Penzance heading home, things are very different up at Crabstock Manor – and whether Lady Crabstock needs our help or not, three cats have been horribly murdered and so far someone has got away with it.'

'What do you think we should do next?' asked Tilly. 'It looks like being a Cornish Christmas for us if we're going to try and solve the murders.'

'Well, at least we have a nice place to stay, and Christmas dinner up at the Atlantic Inn is bound to be a high point. But we'll have to return to Crabstock Manor before then, and without the Bunns knowing anything about it – which means we have to trust someone to help us get in there.'

'I know he's on the suspects list, but what about Sooty Perkins?' Tilly suggested. 'He's been very helpful so far. Do you think we can trust him?'

'I think we'll have to. I wonder if the Bunns are going Christmas shopping? We could do with them being away from the manor for a bit so we can have a good look round. Maybe we could have another chat with Lady Crabstock once her bodyguards are out of the way. Let's go and find Sooty. He might have some ideas on how we can get into the manor unnoticed.'

They found him in the hotel bar, up to his neck in wrapping paper and Sellotape, and Tilly was particularly impressed with the swearing that accompanied his endeavours. He looked up as they joined him at the table. 'Can't find the end to the bloody tape. Not my thing, really, but I promised them up the Atlantic that I'd do these up for the party tonight. Marlon's being Santa Claws again this year, and we're 'avin a live band. Should be a good night if you're looking for something to do to get you in the mood for Christmas, and the whole village will be turnin' out for it.'

Tilly clapped her paws with excitement. 'I love a party! What sort of band are they having?'

'They call themselves The Wooden 'Arts,' replied Sooty. 'Elvis lookalikes, although none of them can sing, but they make a lot of noise which is the main thing for a party. The drummer's good when 'e's not drinkin', but the rest of them are what I'd call bloody terrible.'

'Why don't they book a good band for the party?' asked Hettie, searching for the end to Sooty's Sellotape.

'No point 'avin a good band up there on a party night. They just need a band they can 'ave a good laarf at. As long as the ale flows, that'll be a cracking night, an' no need for serious music.'

Sooty's remarks reminded Hettie of her band days and how upset she had got when the crowd that had turned out to see her had talked and shouted through some of her finest songs, joining in on the choruses and turning her finely tuned performances into a free for all. Clearly, The Wooden Hearts had no such concerns.

'Would it be the sort of party that the Bunns might come to?' asked Hettie hopefully.

'Hevva will be there. 'E comes to all the parties up the Atlantic. Struts around like lord of the manor, 'e does, an' likes to be noticed. Saffron sometimes comes up but 'e don't like 'er mixin' with the rest of us, so 'e might make 'er stay behind at the manor.'

It was Hettie's turn to clap her paws together. 'Perfect. I'm afraid we'll have to give the party a miss, Sooty. We've got some work to do tonight. It's a shame,' she lied. 'I'm sorry to miss The Wooden Hearts.' Tilly caught on quickly, and although she was genuinely disappointed at missing out on an evening up at the Atlantic, she knew that they had much more pressing matters. 'Would it be possible to borrow your map of the manor?' asked Hettie, as Tilly assisted Sooty with his wrapping by holding her paw down on the paper.

'Of course you can, although it's a bit out of date. That map was drawn up in the old glory days when Cornish manor 'ouses was some of the finest in the country.' Sooty reached behind the bar and returned with the plan. 'There you are, but don't you go doin' anything dangerous. Hevva Bunn don't take prisoners.

'E can be a nasty piece of work at the best of times.'

After seeing the Bunns in action, Hettie and Tilly had no doubt that a planned assault on the manor would be dangerous. They were out of their depth in a land where survival was the only true force, and logic had very little to do with anything.

# CHAPTER EIGHTEEN

They spent the afternoon looking round some of the village shops, buying small gifts for each other to exchange on Christmas Day. Hettie also decided to invest in a pair of torches, thinking that they may need them later. It was cold but sunny, and the village bustled with festive cheer. A brass band had set up on the harbour head, conducted by a bespectacled cat who had to stand on several fish boxes to be seen by his players. A tractor was blocking most of the road, while several enthusiastic villagers decorated it with holly and bright red streamers; the tractor pulled a small cart boasting an impressive throne, and was soon to be inhabited by Marlon Brandish, who was doing his best to squeeze into last year's Santa Claws costume. For some reason, the costume seemed to have shrunk, and only the cats around him – tugging and pulling as hard as they dare – suspected that it was due to his increase in size.

The bakers was the busiest shop on the harbour, its windows piled high with seasonal treats: mince pies; Christmas puddings; chocolate logs; novelty snow cat biscuits; and several beautifully decorated Christmas cakes. Hettie and Tilly joined the queue, hoping to stock up on some treats and feeling a little homesick for their own town and Betty and Beryl Butter's pie and pastry shop. As they emerged, laden down with some of their favourites, the brass band struck up with a well-known carol, causing a little confusion for those who had gathered round to sing; the trombones appeared to be playing quite a different tune to the trumpet section, and to make matters worse, the conductor hadn't noticed and seemed to be waving his baton in a world of his own.

The festive cacophony of sound became more pronounced when a group of suited and booted cats emerged from the Harbour Inn and began to sing sea shanties, accompanied by an elderly female cat on a Bontempi organ. The organist glared across the harbour at the brass band, and Hettie and Tilly watched with interest as the tension mounted and the battle of the Christmas entertainers reached fever pitch. The conductor was eventually toppled from his fish boxes by one of the more well-built members of the Crispy Cringles Male Cat Choir, but the onset of physical violence did nothing to dampen the festive spirit of the shoppers, who took sides and cheered along as teeth flew and ears were bitten.

Unbeknown to Hettie and Tilly, the Porthladle Christmas Riot was an annual event, attracting cats from all over Cornwall, which explained why Tiffy Fluff – the well-known local broadcaster – was poised with microphone and camera, ready to rush her report into the teatime news. With choir and band licking their wounds, and the Bontempi and two tubas rescued from the muddy waters of the inner harbour, peace was restored and the entertainers trudged home, battle-sore and weary but determined to meet up later as friends at the Atlantic Inn's party. Hettie lifted her nose in response to an unmistakable temptation. 'Fish and chips,' she said, looking about for the source of her interest. 'There it is – let's take some back to the hotel for tea.'

The fish and chip shop was a far cry from Elsie Haddock's fish emporium back in the town, where chips were large or small and the only fish on offer was cod or haddock. Elsie had resisted becoming a general fast-food outlet and had stuck to plain but nourishing fish and chips; her Cornish counterpart couldn't have been more different.

Arnold Fritter had left his native Porkshire to seek his fortune in the fish and chip trade, armed only with a fish slice and a block of lard. It was luck rather than judgement that had brought him to Porthladle to visit a sick aunt, who obligingly died soon afterwards, willing him her small terraced house tucked away in a little street just off the harbour. Within days of the funeral, Arnold had turned his aunt's old front room into a place completely dedicated to deep fat frying. First came straightforward fish and chips, but it wasn't long before he began to add to his range. Arnold was of the opinion that if you couldn't dip it in batter, it wasn't worth eating, and his popularity spread – around the village at first, and then to visitors who would purchase coach tickets especially to savour his crispy fried bits.

The sign outside his shop boasted that he served award-winning fish and chips, and although no one was quite sure where the award had come from, the list of possibilities to be found in his shop was impressive if a little peculiar. Tilly began to read the menu, a note of bewilderment in her voice. 'Battered chocolate mice, mango fritters, battered Swiss roll, octopus fritters, ice cream fritters, banana fritters, pea fritters, duck fri . . .'

'Quick!' said Hettie, pushing Tilly behind the menu board. 'It's Saffron Bunn – she's coming out of the chip shop. She mustn't see us or she'll tell Hevva we're still here and that will put them on their guard.'

They crammed themselves unceremoniously into the middle of Arnold Fritter's 'A' board as Saffron emerged from the shop and stopped to exchange niceties with the chemist, who was cleaning a little seagull present off her window. 'Damn birds!' the chemist exclaimed. 'Fit for nothin' but roastin'. Are you goin' up the Atlantic tonight, Saffron?'

Hettie and Tilly moved themselves and Arnold Fritter's 'A' board closer to Saffron, waiting for her reply, and were rewarded for their quick thinking. 'I'm goin' up for an hour or two with 'Evva, but I can't stay long as 'Er Ladyship might need somethin'. She don't take kindly to bein' left these days on account of Christmas Paws bein' about. I'm fetchin' us a bit of tea, as I shan't 'ave time to cook.'

The chemist splashed her sponge back into her bucket. 'I'll see you up there for a bit, then. Bye now.'

Saffron waved and turned back to the harbour with her tea tucked under her arm, then walked briskly in the direction of the coastal path. Hettie and Tilly fell out of the 'A' board, much to the amusement of some of Arnold Fritter's customers who had watched the board move subtly from chip shop to chemist and back.

'We'd better get a move on,' said Hettie. 'Let's grab some fish and chips and eat them on the way back to the hotel. We need to stake out the manor and wait for the Bunns to leave so that we can have a good look round.'

Arnold Fritter wasn't in the mood for fast service. Spotting two new faces, he spent some time regaling them with his family history, including a lengthy comparison between the Porkshire Dales and the Cornish coast. Tilly ordered cod and chips twice while Hettie did her best to look interested, hoping that Arnold Fritter would run out of steam. Ten minutes later, they fought their way to freedom with two hot parcels, having avoided all recommendations for the more unusual battered items, and succumbing only to a sprinkling of crispy bits on their chips.

The food was excellent, and there was nothing left but a pile of greasy paper by the time they reached the An Murdress Hotel. Sooty's bar was in full swing as they made their way upstairs, and Hettie breathed a sigh of relief that they were saved from engaging in any further banter; she was keen to get along to Crabstock without meeting the Bunns coming the other way. Back in their room, they busied themselves with choosing dark clothes, wellingtons and the pair of torches they'd bought from the harbour. Tilly rolled up the map that Sooty had leant them and tucked it inside her greatcoat, adding an assortment of festive biscuits to her pockets for emergencies. Both cats crammed bobble hats on their heads and made their way downstairs, past the bar and out onto the cliff road. They passed the Atlantic, pulling their collars up to avoid recognition, and walked on towards Crabstock Manor.

The road was dark and full of puddles, and the wind rose with the incoming tide. The cold was raw against their faces, and at times it was hard to progress more than one or two steps before they were buffeted off course. The landscape was wild and unsympathetic to their mission, and Tilly couldn't help but think that the plan that Hettie had set in motion was a little incomplete. Resting for a moment to catch her breath, she decided to offer her concerns. 'Even if the Bunns do go out together, how will we get into the manor?'

Hettie rubbed her eyes with her paw, trying to shield them from the wind which had now developed into a stinging, icy rain. 'I have no idea,' she said defensively. 'We'll just have to find a way if we're ever to get to the bottom of what's going on.' The wind and rain carried her words away and they trudged on towards the manor house, squinting into the dark for any sign of the Bunns. Eventually, they reached the driveway and left the path to pick their way towards the house under the cover of a rhododendron hedge. The ground was sodden and

175

muddy, and Tilly tripped over what appeared to be a stone sticking out of the earth. Hettie helped her back onto her feet and was just about to lead on when she noticed that they were surrounded by stones. Taking the torch from her pocket, she shone the light at close range onto the obstructions. 'Well, that's all we need!' she mumbled. 'You seem to have stumbled on the final resting place for the whole of the bloody Crabstocks!'

Tilly gasped in horror as her own torch took in the scene. 'Look over there! It just got worse.'

Hettie picked her way through the gravestones in the direction of Tilly's torch beam, and there on the edge of the burial plots was a newly dug grave, the soil piled high next to the hole. The friends stared down into the earth, and Hettie's torch beam revealed that the grave was beginning to fill with water. 'Looks like we may be too late. I assume that this is a little Christmas present for Lady Crabstock-Hinge.'

'Singe,' said Tilly, shivering.

Their thoughts were interrupted by a noise from the driveway, and they switched off their torches and crept back towards the line of rhododendrons. They were close to the house now, and watched as Hevva Bunn emerged from the front door and paced up and down. 'Come on, get yourself out here!' he shouted as Saffron Bunn hurried out, still buttoning her coat. 'Night will be gone by the time you've finished preenin'. Get locked up an' we'll get on before this weather gets any worse.'

Hettie and Tilly held their breath in the shrubbery as the Bunns prepared to make their way to the Atlantic Inn. Before they left, the bit of luck that Hettie always hoped for came her way: Saffron banged the front door shut behind her, turning the key in the lock; reaching down, she appeared to slide the key under one of the giant stone crabs that formed the ornamental welcoming committee at the door of Crabstock Manor. The couple made their way arm in arm past their unseen visitors, still crouching silently in the rhododendrons. Hettie waited for them to reach the end of the driveway, then wasted no time in climbing the steps to the front door, with Tilly following warily behind.

'Yes!' said Hettie, triumphantly recovering the key. 'That's the best bit of luck we've had in this case.'

Tilly, still suffering from her fall and the shock of the open grave, was slightly less enthusiastic about the word 'luck'; the thought of spending any more time in the confines of Crabstock Manor would never be top of her Christmas wish list, but she had to agree that things finally seemed to be going their way. Hettie unlocked the door, replacing the key under the crab, and briefly looked back down the driveway to make sure that they really were alone. Pushing the door open, the cats crept inside, taking care not to make any noise until they'd established their next course of action. The house was in darkness and the giant staircase reared up at them from the hallway. Hettie risked her torch and signalled to Tilly to follow her upstairs to the first landing. 'I think we should try and find Lady Crabstock's room,' she whispered. 'We may be too late to save her, but it's a good place to start.'

Turning right at the top of the stairs, they located the door which had previously led them through to Lady Crabstock's rooms. Faced with a corridor of possibilities, Hettie chose the second door on the right and gently turned the doorknob. The door resisted and there was no sign of a key. Deflated, she moved on to the next door, and this time she was successful. Before them was Lady Crabstock's giant four-poster bed, lit dimly by a small bedside lamp and shrouded in net curtains as before – but it was the smell that instantly caught Tilly's attention. Her eyes focused on the dining table to the right of the bed, and there were the remnants of a hurriedly finished meal.

It was hard to see if the bed was occupied and Hettie decided to throw caution to the wind. 'Your Ladyship,' she began, speaking to the curtains, 'I wonder if we might have another word with you?' There was no reply, so Hettie moved closer to the bed.

'Your Ladyship?' she repeated, this time with more urgency. There was still no reply. Seizing the corner of one of the curtains, Hettie drew it back and stared at the empty space where she had expected to find the corpse of Lady Crabstock-Singe. Relieved but puzzled, she shone her torch round the rest of the room. 'What the hell has been going on in here? Look at this – it's that bloody Christmas tree we saw them lugging back here this afternoon.' The tree was set up in the bay window overlooking the sea, and the decorations were a work in progress; a number of glass baubles hung from the branches, with more waiting in boxes underneath, and there were several wrapped presents on one of the chairs. The whole scene looked perfectly normal for the evening of the 23rd of December.

Hettie began to panic, thinking that Her Ladyship would return to her room at any moment and treat them as intruders – which, after all, they were. But it was Tilly's observations regarding the dining table that temporarily put their minds at rest. 'Either Lady Crabstock is quite greedy or the Bunns have had their tea in here,' she said, taking a closer look at the table. 'Look – they've left their fish and chip papers and two slices of bread and butter, and that teapot is still warm. I think that this room has been taken over by Hevva and Saffron.'

Hettie joined Tilly at the table, noticing that it had

clearly been vacated in a hurry. 'It looks to me as if the Bunns have got a bit above themselves. Perhaps their takeover of Crabstock Manor is complete, but where is Lady Crabstock? She was here in this room yesterday. We both saw her, and she was giving orders from that very bed as if she was still very much in charge.'

Tilly thought for a moment. 'Maybe we haven't actually met Lady Crabstock yet,' she offered. 'We didn't exactly see her, and when we did see her she didn't want to see us. Maybe if we *had* seen her, she wouldn't have sent us away. She did ask to see us in the first place, and she went to a lot of trouble to get us here.'

Hettie slumped down on one of the dining chairs, trying to hang on to Tilly's reasoning. 'So what are you saying?' she asked, slightly irritated.

'I'm saying that the cat in the bed yesterday might not have been Lady Crabstock, and that we've been tricked into believing it was.'

Hettie stood up. 'So who was it? It can't have been Saffron – she brought us in here, and Hevva was on his way out when we arrived back from the village. There must be another cat involved, and one we know nothing about – which means we might not be on our own in here tonight. And let's not forget that if it *wasn't* Lady Crabstock, she may be lying dead somewhere in this godforsaken house, waiting to join her relatives

180

out in the front garden as part of the landscaping.'

'Maybe it was Christmas Paws,' said Tilly, trying to be helpful.

'You do have a point there.' Hettie looked under the four poster, beginning her search for Lady Crabstock. 'Christmas Paws is the only other cat we've seen here, and she could easily be playing the bit parts under the Bunns' direction, but she's not hiding under this bed.' Dusting herself down and removing a cobweb from her bobble hat, Hettie knew that there was no time to waste. Saffron had made it clear that she would be returning early from the Atlantic party, supposedly to look after Lady Crabstock, and there was very little time left for them to search the manor. 'Let's have a quick look at Sooty's map,' she said. 'If you're right and we haven't met Lady Crabstock, she may be a prisoner somewhere in the house – that's if she's not dead. But why would you dig a grave if someone *wasn't* dead? It seems to me that we're just too late to save the Crabstocks from extinction.'

Tilly opened the map on the table and the two cats pored over it, looking for possible areas of interest. 'Most of the secret passageways seem to link the big rooms,' Tilly observed. 'The best places to hide things are in the cellars or in those rooms near the kitchen. I think with the time we have left we should forget about the posh bits of the house and take a closer look downstairs.'

Hettie agreed and they set off back to the main staircase, watchful of any movement or sound in the old house. They turned into the kitchen corridor and systematically opened the doors, peering into all the rooms. Each was neglected, and stacked with the abandoned days of domestic glory that the manor had once enjoyed: a butler's pantry without the butler; a once-neat housekeeper's sitting room, piled high with greying laundry and giant cooking pots; a boot room with brushes lying forgotten under polish-stained benches; and a dairy, inhabited by several redundant butter churns. It occurred to Hettie that if they were looking for the ghosts of Crabstock Manor, they had found them in the very fabric of these sad and lifeless walls.

The kitchen was tidy and unwelcoming. The fire in the grate sulked and smoked as the wind roared down the chimney, doing its best to deaden any sign of life. Hettie shone her torch into the corner where they had seen the ghost of Christmas Paws. There was the door that Sooty had told them led down to the old wine cellar, and eventually to the sea. In the opposite corner was another door which they hadn't noticed during their previous visits. 'Let's take a look in there,' she said, moving across the kitchen and lifting the latch. She gasped. 'Well – just take a look at this lot!'

Tilly's eyes threatened to pop out of her head at the sight before them. 'I don't think I've ever seen so much food in one room,' she said, allowing her torch to sweep the shelves. 'This must be the larder, but look at the hams hanging from those nasty hooks! That's the biggest turkey I've ever seen, and that pudding's the size of a football!'

'It seems to me that the Bunns are planning a very fine Christmas indeed, unless Lady Crabstock-Twinge has invited the whole of Porthladle to Christmas dinner here at the manor.' Hettie took in the size of a whole Cornish Brie and a giant slab of Cruncher Cheddar. Tempted, but determined to resist the Aladdin's cave of festive comestibles, she shut the door on the larder. 'I don't think we can put it off any longer,' she said. 'Let's take a look at the other door that leads to the cellar. Saffron could be back at any minute.'

The door was locked. 'Bugger!' said Tilly, then brightened. 'If Saffron leaves a key under a stone at the front door, she's probably left one for this door somewhere simple, too.'

The two cats swept the kitchen with the beams of their torches, looking for a likely hiding place. Tilly launched herself into an inspection of the drawers in the dresser, while Hettie focused on various pots on the mantelpiece, but there was no sign anywhere of the cellar key. 'Wait a minute,' said Hettie, returning to the door. 'You said simple, so let me see.' Reaching up, she ran her paw along the ledge of the door frame; suddenly, there was a resounding clink that seemed to echo through the house as the dislodged key rattled onto the kitchen's flagstone floor.

Hettie and Tilly waited in silence, afraid of being discovered at any moment by an unseen presence, but nothing happened. 'Come on,' said Hettie, recovering herself. 'Let's get this over with.'

She unlocked the door quickly, replacing the key on the ledge, and pulled the door open onto a flight of worn stone steps. Instantly they could hear the sea below them, growing steadily louder as they descended into the bowels of Crabstock Manor, their torch beams almost meaningless in the vast cavern before them.

# CHAPTER NINETEEN

The pre-Christmas celebrations were not going too well up at the Atlantic Inn. Marlon Brandish's makeshift sleigh had broken down shortly after leaving the harbour; Marlon himself had broken down just outside Sooty's hotel, due to the astonishing amount of Doom Bar he had consumed. To make matters worse, Boy Cockle had had one of his turns after smoking too much catnip, and had had to be airlifted by a helicopter from the Cold Nose Airbase to the cottage hospital at Fowlmouth. Sooty had done his best to pacify the village's kitten population by explaining that Santa Claws was overtired and wouldn't be putting in an appearance any time soon, and The Wooden Hearts hadn't shown up at all. The Crispy Cringle Male Cat Choir had seized the opportunity to provide alternative entertainment, but had been beaten to the Atlantic's stage area by six members of the Porthladle Brass Band, all of whom had taken strong drink.

The fight started in the lounge bar but quickly spread to every corner of the inn. Tiffy Fluff, who was supposed to have announced the arrival of Santa in her official capacity as village celebrity, found herself pinned to the specials board, with the headphones which she used as winter earmuffs dangling around her neck. The Christmas tree which had looked a picture earlier was now a source of weaponry as baubles and plastic icicles were hurled through the air; Loveday Whisk – drinking a Vimto at the time – was an early casualty and had been temporarily knocked unconscious by a flying tankard.

It was the height of misfortune for Hettie and Tilly that the Atlantic's party had to be abandoned only half an hour after it had begun. Already in the foulest of moods, Hevva and Saffron Bunn began to make their way back to Crabstock Manor much sooner than anyone had expected.

# CHAPTER TWENTY

The walls in the cellar were dripping with green slime and the old brick floor was slippery. The smell of damp was overpowering, and the presence of the sea only a few yards away crashed into their minds as a yet unseen terror. They could see very little of what the cellar offered – just dark corners and recesses leading from one section to another, stretching out towards the roar of the ocean. Tilly reached for Hettie's paw in the darkness. 'I don't think we should be here. I'm frightened. We've done our best and now I think we should go while we still can.'

It was rare for Tilly to give in to her fears. Life had dealt her some painful blows but she had always looked on the bright side and could never be described as a quitter. Hettie understood this, as they had shared so many scrapes together, and now – whatever secrets the cellar held – she knew that this was one mystery which she was also very happy to leave unsolved. If Lady Crabstock's body was awaiting burial somewhere in that subterranean hellhole, then so be it. 'You're right,' she said, leading them back to the stairs. 'Let's get out of here.'

They climbed the steps and had almost reached the top when they heard raised voices coming from the kitchen. 'Even if you tried 'ard, you couldn't be any more stupid than you are now!' shouted Hevva Bunn, following the words with a resounding slap. 'An' there's plenty more where that came from. Leaving the manor open to anyone who cares to call, with things as they are – it's you who needs lockin' up.'

'But 'Evva, I tell you I *did* lock the front door, I know I did,' whimpered Saffron as another blow rained down on her.

'You can get yourself down that cellar while I check the rest of the house, and God 'elp you if we've 'ad visitors. 'Ere's somethin' to 'elp you on your way!'

'Please, 'Evva – not your belt! I was so cut up last time,' Saffron pleaded as the belt buckle landed first across her back, then across the side of her face.

Hettie and Tilly held their breath, wanting to intervene but knowing that their presence would only make things worse. Instinctively, they backed down the steps into the cellar as the tirade of abuse continued from the kitchen. The sobbing went on for some time, although the beating had stopped. Hettie knew that they would have to find a safe place to hide. Moving further into the warren of rooms, they settled on a stall tucked away from the main floor area, with a collection of gardening tools, an old lawnmower and a pile of abandoned sacks for company. The two cats settled themselves under the sacks and waited silently in the dark.

What came next was totally unexpected. Peeping out from the sacking, Hettie and Tilly stared in horror as a beam of light progressed across the cellar floor, stopping inches away from them. The light turned as if searching for something, and the two friends saw Christmas Paws in the full glare of the lantern she carried, her face contorted like some horrific mask from a bad joke shop. Tilly's heart began to beat so loudly that she thought she would give them away. They shrank back into the sacking, hoping that the ghost would move on – and she did. Seconds later, the cellar was filled with a pitiful wailing, the same noise they'd heard when the ghost had appeared in the kitchen.

After some time, the wailing stopped and all was silent except for the occasional crashing wave. Hettie and Tilly were about to emerge from their sacking when the hideous form of Christmas Paws loomed out of the darkness and seemed to move towards the cellar stairs. Hettie waited for several minutes, then signalled to Tilly to stay put and fumbled her way back to the steps, using the slimy walls to guide her in the dark. On reaching the top of the steps, she listened at the door for any sound coming from the kitchen, but all was quiet. Taking a deep breath, she located the latch and gently lifted it, pushing the door open at the same time. It was as she had feared and expected – firmly locked from the other side.

She sank to the floor, switching her torch on for comfort. Tilly had ignored her instructions and followed her to the bottom of the steps, and she saw the look of defeat on her friend's face in the torchlight. 'We're locked in, aren't we?' she whispered.

Hettie nodded and joined her back in the cellar. 'Well, this is a fine bloody pickle we're in,' she said, trying to make light of the situation for Tilly's benefit. 'The good news is that all sounds quiet in the Bunns' kitchen, so either Hevva has finished Saffron off or they've patched things up and are finishing the decorations on their Christmas tree in Her Ladyship's room. We have to find a way out of here before we both die of cold or are murdered by Christmas Paws.'

At the mention of the malevolent spirit, the wailing began again – quieter this time, and punctuated by the sound of rattling chains. It occurred to Hettie that Christmas Paws was putting on quite a show for their benefit. Resigned to whatever fate was about to befall

190

them, they adjusted their torches to full beam and went in search of the wailing and clanking. Staying together, they chose a side of the cellar each and shone their lights into every nook and cranny as they moved forward towards the intermittent noise. They passed their earlier refuge and moved on through the discarded detritus of the old manor house – furniture, rolled carpets, frames without paintings, a rusty suit of armour, shards of stained glass that had once formed pictures of brave endeavours. All seemed to be tainted with the creeping death that had infected the ancient walls, both physically and spiritually.

Entirely without warning, the cellar became an open-mouthed cave, leaving the formal structure of the house behind. In front of them, the Atlantic Ocean pounded the shore. The cave was separated from the sea by a grille of iron, designed to keep the manor safe from unwanted ship-borne visitors but open enough to allow the full blast of the elements in. Hettie remembered what Sooty had said about access to the house from outside in the days when the sea hadn't claimed so much of the land. She could taste the salt as they stared out at the waves thrashing on the sand only yards away from them, and she knew that there would be no escape in that direction.

The floor of the cave was littered with crab pots, nets and the remnants of an old rowing boat. Tilly shone her torch around the walls and located several barrels and an assortment of waterproof clothing similar to Sooty's fishing outfit. Raising the beam higher, she found a web of fishing nets above her head, hooked into the walls like giant hammocks. As her light fell on the nets, the wailing began again, leaving them in no doubt as to where it was coming from.

'It's in those nets!' cried Tilly, dropping her torch in shock.

Hettie swung her beam at the nets and realised to her horror that there was something caught up in the webbing, and the blood-curdling noise it was making suggested that it was very much alive and in need of assistance. The two cats sprang into action and hauled one of the barrels under the nets. Hettie climbed onto it to reach the hook that the net was fixed to; dislodging it, she took the strain as Tilly steadied it from below, and the pathetic bundle was lowered gently to the floor of the cave. Slowly and carefully, they untangled the net using their teeth and claws, but nothing could have prepared them for the bag of bones they eventually released. She was old and grey, and her eyes bulged from their sockets; her bones stood out like tent poles, and her legs were bound in rusty chains which had cut into her fur to reveal the flesh beneath.

She hardly moved as Hettie and Tilly stared down at her, not knowing what to do next for fear of causing her more pain. Tilly reacted first by pulling off her greatcoat and covering her up, remembering the first-aid course that Hettie had sent her on. 'We have to keep her warm,' she said, shivering at the loss of her coat.

'We need to get those chains off her, too. Stay here with her while I go and look for some tools.' Hettie returned to the cellar and made her way back to where they had hidden in the sacks. The garden tools were too big for what she needed but, on closer inspection, she found an old rusted toolbox. Not caring any more about the noise she was making, she emptied the contents onto the floor and sorted through with the torch. Luck was on her side: a pair of hefty wire cutters offered themselves, along with a hammer and an assortment of chisels. She wrapped the tools in a bundle of sacks and made her way back to the cave.

'I think she's dying,' said Tilly, relieved at Hettie's return. 'She seems to be gasping for breath and she looks so frightened. I think we're going to lose her.'

'Not if I can help it,' Hettie replied, setting about the chains with the cutter. The elderly cat lay still as her manacles were gently removed. Tilly pulled one of her best handkerchiefs from her cardigan pocket and ripped it in two, binding the cat's injured paws where the chains had cut into her. Hettie arranged some of the sacks into a makeshift bed tucked away from the blast of the sea, and the two cats lifted their patient onto them. Tilly retrieved her coat, grateful for the warmth as Hettie tucked a blanket of sacking round the elderly cat, who had now closed her eyes.

'Someone needs to be punished for this,' said Hettie angrily. 'And whatever happens, I'm going to make sure of it. She's been left to die here, starved in this freezing cold place, chained like a wild animal and left without hope. What sort of maniac does that?'

Tilly stared down at the elderly cat and had no answer but her tears. She wept quietly for the hopelessness of their situation, and their inability to do anything about it.

An hour past as the three cats huddled together for warmth. The old cat's breathing had improved and she began to show signs of life, murmuring disconnected words which gradually became more lucid. 'You must leave before she returns,' she whispered.

Tilly moved closer to hear more, but the cat began to sob and her words were lost. 'Please don't cry,' she said. 'We're here to help. My name's Tilly and this is my friend, Hettie. Would you like to tell us your name?'

'Eloise,' came the feeble reply.

'It's Lady Crabstock!' Tilly gasped.

Hettie stared down at the desperately wasted body shrouded in sacking, suddenly more horrific than ever now that its nobility had been established. 'Lady

Crabstock,' she began, 'you sent for us. We're from the No. 2 Feline Detective Agency.'

Eloise Crabstock struggled to sit up as her eyes adjusted to the light of Tilly's torch. 'You are too late to save me, but you must try and save yourselves. She'll come back soon. She's promised to kill me tomorrow if I don't die tonight, and she'll kill you, too, if she finds you. There's nothing you can do. The prophesy will be fulfilled.'

'Who is going to kill you?' asked Hettie, knowing the answer already.

'Christmas Paws,' came the expected reply. 'She's murdered all my family one by one. Now it's time for me to die and the curse will finally leave the manor.'

Hettie could see that Lady Crabstock was far too weak and frightened for any meaningful discussion on the capability of ghosts to torture and murder, so she decided to turn the subject away from the Crabstock curse to more urgent matters. 'How long have you been down here?'

Lady Crabstock looked bewildered at the question but did her best to respond. 'I'm not really sure. It was just after I'd seen Christmas, the same day I wrote to you. I was ill with a cold. Marlon took the letter and I went to bed. Oh, I'm sorry – I just can't remember anything after that. I've been in this cave for a long time, I think. I woke up on the floor in chains, I remember that. She came to me and bound me up in

195

the nets. She visits me when it gets dark. At first I cried for water and food, but she laughed at me. Then I just gave up.'

Lady Crabstock began to sob again, reminding Hettie of just how fragile she was. It seemed pointless to go over what had happened when they needed to make some sort of attempt at escape. Tilly had been spot on about their first meeting with her, but who had they spoken to through the veil of bed curtains? Had Hevva Bunn doubled back and slipped into his mistress's bedsheets? Or was Christmas Paws more earthly than her legend suggested? The really big question was where the Bunns fitted in. They must be aware that Lady Crabstock had gone missing. They'd taken over her room and Saffron had been told to check the cellar, and her conversation with the chemist that afternoon had inferred that she was still looking after her employer. Nothing made any real sense, but clearly Christmas Paws was building to her final act of murder, regardless of who else was involved.

The new bout of sobbing had exhausted Eloise Crabstock. She settled back on her sacking and closed her eyes, and Hettie called Tilly over to the pile of nets that had so recently imprisoned her. 'Give me a hand to put these back up there on that hook. We'll wrap the chains up in them to make it look like she's still caught in the nets. If the ghostly Miss Paws decides to pay another visit, she'll think that Lady Crabstock has finally died.' The two cats worked hard to put the web of nets back on the hooks and were satisfied that all looked as they had found it.

'It's getting really cold in here,' said Tilly, pulling her coat around her. 'I think we should find a better place in the cellar, away from the sea, until we decide what to do.'

Hettie agreed. Leaving Tilly with Lady Crabstock, she returned to the cellar to scout out a place of safety. The beam of her torch was becoming weaker as it played on the mountain of discarded furniture, eventually coming to rest on an old oak dresser tucked away in a recess. She had a brief pang for home as she pictured the staff sideboard in their little room, where Tilly kept everything that had a purpose in life. On closer inspection, the old dresser was perfect: the bottom part of it had a giant cupboard with two doors which would make a perfect sanctuary for Lady Crabstock while they plotted their escape.

She returned triumphant to the cave, and she and Tilly carried their patient on her sacking to her new hideaway in the cellar. Having installed Eloise Crabstock in the dresser, Hettie and Tilly settled themselves on a bit of old carpet to take a look at Sooty's map again. The cellar was marked, and in the failing light of Hettie's torch they noticed that – as well as the entrance now cut off by the sea – there was a coal chute that came into the cellar from outside.

'Let's take a look,' said Hettie, getting to her feet. 'It looks like it's under the kitchen.'

They made their way back to the stairs which led up to the kitchen, pausing briefly to check for any sound from above. 'Look,' whispered Tilly. 'There's the coal heap and there's rain coming in from outside.' With a leap that surprised herself, Tilly clambered onto the pile of coal and worked her way to the top of the stack.

'What can you see?' demanded Hettie, impatient for news.

There was a cracking sound, followed by an avalanche of coal as Tilly tumbled back down to the cellar floor. A little dazed, she sat for a moment before reporting her findings. 'There's a wooden cover over the coal hole, but it's rotten and I managed to pull a plank off before I fell. I think I might be able to squeeze through it if I took my coat off.'

Hettie was pleased that at last they had a chance to put the horrors of Crabstock Manor behind them. 'One of us should go for help. We'll never get Lady Crabstock out that way. I think we're going to have to trust Sooty Perkins.'

Tilly agreed and got to her feet, taking her coat off. 'I think I'll have to go. You won't fit through the hole, but you'll have to pass me my coat or I'll freeze out there.'

Before Hettie could argue, Tilly had scaled the coal

heap once again and was busily squeezing herself out. Hettie followed her to the top of the stack and posted her coat through the hole. 'Good luck and be careful,' she said, then she lost her balance, too, and slid to the bottom of the coal mountain. Picking herself up, she returned to the oak dresser to check on the patient. She was sleeping, and for a moment all was peaceful in the cellar below Crabstock Manor.

# CHAPTER TWENTY-ONE

Tilly shivered. The cellar had been cold, but that was nothing compared to the icy blast that she found herself in now, and she knew that she would have to keep moving if her joints weren't to seize up altogether. The manor glared down at her like an unbreachable fortress of evil. She felt so small as she battled against the wind, staying close to the walls of the house for shelter until she had reached the driveway. She chose to pick her way through the burial ground rather than use the path to the road, just in case she was spotted by the Bunns from one of the windows.

Eventually, reaching the cliff road, she looked back at the house and was pleased to see that it was all in darkness. Pulling her hat down almost to her nose, she struck out for the village. Every bone in her body hurt. The extreme cold was taking its toll and, to make matters worse, it had begun to snow – gently at first, filling the night sky with white dancing feathers as they fell to earth, followed by a relentless torrent of thick flakes which settled quickly on the ground. Tilly's already slow progress was almost at a standstill. The storm was blinding her and the wind had picked up even more, blasting the snow into thick sculptures which wrapped themselves around the trees and the drystone walls that marked the road to the village. She could see nothing ahead, and dragged herself blindly forward into the blizzard.

She was aware that the sea was on her left, but it was her only reference point. The snow was getting deeper and had reached the top of her wellingtons, filling them with icy cold water as it melted and making it even more difficult for her to put one foot in front of the other. She cried out with the pain of her frozen toes, and her tears turned to ice across her nose. She was exhausted, and on the verge of falling asleep as she walked. She concentrated hard on staying awake, resisting the temptation to give in to her tiredness and lie down in the snow. In the bad days, when she was homeless, she used to shelter on a shelf in an old shed during the winter, and she remembered that she would sing to stay awake for fear of freezing to death like so many other homeless cats had done. With a deep breath, she launched herself into a medley of

Christmas carols, not caring how she ordered the verses or the tunes. She bellowed them out across the snowy landscape, determined to keep going. The snow began to ease off and the wind dropped, making Tilly's lonely voice sound rather strange and unearthly in the silence. Gradually, even the sea calmed itself into a gentle caressing of the shoreline as the tide pulled out in deference to the snow-covered sand.

There was no need for her torch now. The snow lit her way with absolute clarity, and the slightest hint of a twinkly light in the distance gave her hope that the village was now in sight. She had no energy left, but she knew at this point that failure was not an option. She dug her paws deeply into the pockets of her greatcoat and was rewarded with the Christmas biscuits which she had pocketed for emergencies – still there, if a little fragmented by recent traumas. The biscuits lasted seconds but the effect of the sugar was life-saving. With a new resolve and a determination to complete her mission, she pushed on, dragging herself through the snow until she had reached the first cottages at the boundary of the village.

She remembered falling flat on her face in the snow with exhaustion, but had no recollection of the village cats who carried her up to the Atlantic Inn and placed her in front of a roaring fire in the public bar. Sooty Perkins' face was the first she recognised as he trickled small amounts of brandy into her mouth. She sneezed and sent the liquid into the fire, suddenly realising that she was surrounded by several wide-eyed cats, all looking on with great concern.

'Thank goodness!' said Sooty. 'We thought you was a goner when they brought you in. Frozen solid, you were.'

It took Tilly a little while to get her bearings, but the warmth of the fire and Sooty's encouraging voice gradually brought her to her senses. She knew there was something urgent at the back of her mind, but couldn't quite remember what it was. Sooty coaxed her into taking some sips of hot, sweet tea, and Loveday Whisk gently massaged her frozen paws back to life. 'Fancy bein' out on a night like this,' she said. 'And what about your friend? I 'ope she's not out there in all this weather.'

Tilly choked on her tea, spilling it down the front of her festive cardigan. 'Hettie!' she cried. 'She's locked in the cellar with poor Lady Crabstock and Christmas Paws!'

All eyes turned to Tilly, waiting for her to continue, but Sooty saw her distress and interrupted. 'Now then, I think you've got yourself confused. Lady Crabstock will be tucked up at the manor, safe and sound. She's not the sort to go cavorting in cellars.' The rest of the assembled company laughed at Sooty's words, all except Tilly who could feel hot tears of frustration and embarrassment welling up in her eyes.

She struggled to her feet. 'Please listen to me!' she cried as Tiffy Fluff pushed her way to the front, all but forcing her microphone up Tilly's nose in her eagerness for an exclusive. 'Lady Crabstock is a prisoner at Crabstock Manor. Hettie and I found her chained and tied up in nets in the cave under the house. She's so ill she's probably going to die, and Hettie is looking after her while I came here for help. We have to do something now or it will be too late.'

Tilly had silenced the crowd, and the urgency in her voice got Sooty's undivided attention at last. 'If they're locked in that old cellar, why don't the Bunns let 'em out? Surely they've got a key? They left the party soon after the fight began. They must 'ave been back at the manor for some time.'

Tilly responded by giving an account of Saffron's beating and the appearance of Christmas Paws, finishing with her escape through the coal chute and her journey through the blizzard into the village. When she'd finished, there was much shaking of heads and murmuring in the crowd, and it was Loveday who spoke first. 'I've been sayin' this all along an' no one would listen. 'Evva Bunn 'as a black 'eart. 'E treats Saffron terrible, an' if 'e's started on 'Er Ladyship we got to get it sorted. 'E's much more frightenin' than Christmas Paws, so come on you lot – get your coats an' let's get ourselves to the manor before it's too late.'

A cheer went up around the bar, but Sooty raised

his paw and called for calm. 'Loveday is right but we 'ave to get organised. The weather's terrible an' it's goin' to take some time to reach the manor on foot on account of the snow. I think what we need is a two-pronged attack.'

Sooty was well respected in the village, and was regarded as a cat with a good head on him. In times of trouble, the villagers would seek him out, knowing that his opinion counted for a great deal and that his wisdom and guidance would be invaluable. Now, they stood as one and waited for direction.

'Salty, I'll need you with me,' Sooty began. 'I think the quickest way to get to the manor is by sea, an' from what Tilly is sayin' we can land in Crabstock Cove an' get in that way, without givin' the game away.'

Tilly interrupted at this point. 'The cave is blocked up with big iron bars.'

Sooty laughed. 'Don't you worry about that. I'll soon 'ave them shifted. A couple of sticks of dynamite will sort that out a treat. Now, where was I? Oh yes, Potsy and Dory, if you can get as many cats together as you can an' get yourselves to the manor by the cliff road, we'll 'ave the front covered as well. Keep yourselves quiet when you get there an' wait for my signal. I'll send up a flare from Crabstock Cove, which will be the signal to take the house. Get started as soon as you can an' arm yourselves for a fight, just in case 'Evva kicks up rough. Loveday, I want you to stay here an' look after Tilly. I think she's 'ad enough for one night.'

Again Tilly interrupted. 'I'd rather come and see it through. I'm feeling much better now.'

Loveday piped up, too. 'You can count me in on your boat trip, Sooty. I'm not missin' out on a proper adventure. Me an' Tilly 'ere can keep your engine running while you an' Salty do the business on the shore.'

Sooty was about to argue but saw the sense in having as many pairs of paws as was available; Lady Crabstock would need special care if they got to her in time. 'OK, you win, but get yourselves wrapped up warm. I've got some spare waterproofs at the 'otel. We can pick them up on our way down to the 'arbour.'

Leaving Potsy and Dory to gather their army together, Sooty Perkins escorted Tilly and Loveday back to his hotel, sending Salty on ahead to fire up the engine on his boat. Tiffy Fluff switched off her tape recorder with satisfaction, knowing she had the scoop of the century, and pulled on her wellingtons in preparation to follow the story to the gates of Crabstock Manor.

# CHAPTER TWENTY-TWO

Back at the hotel, Loveday and Tilly climbed into some of Sooty's old waterproofs, which were far too big for them. Sooty insisted on adding life jackets to their outfits and the three cats set out for the harbour, making slow progress through the snow. Tilly's joints ached from the cold and she stumbled several times before Sooty picked her up and tucked her under his arm, holding Loveday up with his other paw as she slipped and slid on snow which was now beginning to freeze.

The engine of the *Maid of Kelynack* was chugging away by the time they reached the quayside, and Salty waved from the wheelhouse, signalling that he would bring the small punt to the bottom of the harbour steps to transfer them to the boat. Using a single oar,

Salty sculled across to the bottom of the steps where Sooty loaded Tilly and Loveday into the punt. 'Get them over first, Salty. We won't all fit – not with them life jackets takin' up the space.' Salty used his oar to push away from the shore; reaching the *Maid of Kelynack*, he lifted first Loveday and then Tilly up onto the deck of the boat before returning to the shore to collect Sooty.

'Right then,' Sooty said, swinging himself aboard and securing the punt to the back of the boat. 'Let's set you girls to work. We might even make proper sailors of you. Tilly, you get yourself into the wheel'ouse and get that kettle on. Loveday, you take the stern and cast us off. Salty, get yourself to the bow.' Sooty clambered into the wheelhouse, and as the ropes from bow and stern were slipped he steered the boat out of the inner harbour, past the pier and the clock tower on one side and a line of jagged rocks on the other.

The clock tower clunked ten as they headed out to open sea. Tilly, as far as she could remember, had never been on a boat of any sort and found the strange motion rather alarming. She concentrated hard on making four mugs of tea in the tiny galley, fighting the seasickness that was beginning to creep up on her. Loveday joined her and rescued the tea bags from the mugs as Tilly tried several times to spoon in some powdered milk, but most of it ended up on the floor of the galley.

'You don't look too good,' observed Loveday,

locating a tin of chocolate digestives. 'You'll do better if you go out on deck. That 'elps yer to get yer sea legs. 'Ere – take this tea up to Salty.'

Tilly did as she was told and had to agree that the icy blast of fresh air did wonders. The sea was actually quite calm, the moon offered a silver path which stretched out onto the distant horizon, and the stars twinkled in the night sky as bright as she had ever seen them. She made her way to the bow, where Salty stood scouring the shoreline with his binoculars. Grateful for the hot tea, he wrapped his paws around the mug for extra warmth and stared up at the sky. 'That there is the north star,' he said, lifting his head. 'Never brighter than at this time of year. Sailor's friend, she is – leads us 'ome.'

Tilly stared in wonder, quite forgetting her seasickness. 'Have you sailed a lot?' she asked, studying the weather-beaten cat who stood before her.

Salty's face lit up at the question. 'All my life, really. My old dad 'ad a boat, and 'e fished these waters till the great storm took 'im. Took me out as a kitten an' taught me everythin' I know, then when 'e was gone I joined up as a merchant on the big ships out of Fowlmouth. Travelled the world, I did, then when my old ma died I came back 'ere an' teamed up with Sooty an' the *Maid of Kelynack* to get back to proper fishin'. There's a good livin' to be 'ad if you've a fine boat like this one.'

'It's a funny name for a boat.'

'Well, you'll 'ave to mention that to Sooty,' said Salty, laughing. ''E's called 'er after 'is sweet'eart. Been courtin' 'er for years.' Salty took up his binoculars again and directed them at the shore. 'Start bringin' 'er in!' he shouted back to Sooty in the wheelhouse.

Tilly stared at the shore and marvelled at how very different the village looked from the sea – row after row of twinkling cottages, some nestling at sea level and others perched high on the clifftop, their roofs covered in snow. She followed the line of the cliff road and eventually spotted the dark, forbidding outline of Crabstock Manor. She was suddenly engulfed by a great sadness and fear for Hettie, who was still imprisoned within its walls. It was all her fault: she had wanted this Cornish adventure, never dreaming that it could put Hettie in such peril. Her best friend in all the world was captive in a filthy cellar, and at this very moment was probably being tortured by Christmas Paws.

A sudden hive of activity on deck snatched her from her inner turmoil. Sooty emerged from the wheelhouse carrying an anchor attached to a coiled rope. 'I've knocked the engine out and left 'er idlin'. I reckon we're about fifty yards out from Crabstock Cove, so we'll take the punt from 'ere.' Sooty threw the anchor over the side of the boat and waited for it to hit the bottom before securing the rope to the cleat hook on the bow. Checking they had everything they needed for their assault on the shore, Sooty and Salty lowered themselves down into the punt.

Loveday had come up on deck to see them off, and stood with Tilly as the two cats sculled their way to the shore. 'Don't you worry,' she said. 'Sooty will sort it. 'E'll 'ave your friend out of there in no time, an' the village folk will take good care of 'Evva Bunn and put an end to Christmas Paws and 'er antics, you mark my words.'

At the mention of the villagers, Tilly's gaze was directed away from the speeding little boat and towards the clifftop, where a procession of flaming torches made slow progress towards Crabstock Manor. It was clear that Potsy and Dory's army was on its way to the front door of the house. Loveday went back into the wheelhouse and returned seconds later with two sets of binoculars. ''Ere, take these, or you'll miss all the action.'

Tilly raised the binoculars to her eyes and spent some time getting them to focus on the little punt. By the time she had the boat in her sights, it had almost reached the shore. Sooty and Salty leapt into the water and dragged the punt onto the snowy sand, and Tilly watched as they headed towards the cave entrance. She lifted the binoculars to take in the manor house above, and noticed that the stream of torches had disappeared from view. She imagined them assembled outside the front door, waiting for Sooty's signal.

A crack rang out across the night sky as Sooty's dynamite wrenched a hole in the entrance to the cave. Tilly and Loveday reacted by training their binoculars back onto the beach, just in time to see Sooty and Salty disappear inside. The waiting was almost more than Tilly could stand. She was frozen to the spot at the bow of the boat, mentally working her way through every possible bad-news scenario that she could invent. Loveday had returned to the wheelhouse and was nervously crunching her way through the tin of chocolate digestives as the little boat bobbed up and down expectantly. Eventually, there was a movement on the beach and Tilly called to her. 'I think they're out of the cave! Come and see!'

Loveday bustled onto the deck and raised her binoculars. 'Yep, that's them all right. Sooty's carryin' somethin' and puttin' it in the punt, only . . .' Loveday faltered in her commentary.

'Only what?' asked Tilly, becoming visibly distressed.

'Well, I was goin' to say I can't see your friend, but maybe she's gone to join Potsy and Dory. Sooty 'asn't give the signal for them to move yet,' said Loveday, trying to remain positive.

Sooty and Salty made good time returning to their boat, and Tilly and Loveday assisted as they lifted what appeared to be a bundle of sacks onto the deck.

The sacks began to cry, more with relief than pain, as four pairs of eyes stared down in great concern at Lady Eloise Crabstock-Singe. Loveday was the first to speak. 'Your Ladyship, is that really you? What 'ave they done? They'll pay for this, you can be sure of that.'

Eloise Crabstock struggled to sit up and Sooty supported her as she spoke. 'I owe you a great debt,' she said, looking at Tilly, 'but I fear for your friend. She's been taken by Christmas Paws. Christmas came to kill me, but she went mad when she couldn't find me in the nets. Your friend protected me. I was in the dresser, listening. There was a terrible fight, then it all went quiet. I was too weak to move. I'm so sorry.'

Tilly turned away and looked out across the sea, hot tears splashing down onto her paws as she clung to the side of the boat. Why had she left Hettie to face Christmas Paws on her own? Together they might have been strong enough to overcome this malevolent force. Together was how it was supposed to be, but now there was just a hole, a desolate void, a grief unimagined in all her darkest fears.

Loveday and Salty gently lifted Lady Crabstock into the wheelhouse and settled her by the engine for warmth. Sooty stared at the sad, dejected form of Tilly, looking for words of consolation and finding none. He stared back at Crabstock Cove and realised that he hadn't given the flare signal to Potsy and Dory.

It was hard to know what to do: Lady Crabstock was in a bad way and needed a warm bed and plenty of care, but there was unfinished business at Crabstock Manor and the day of reckoning had come. 'Right!' he said, making Tilly jump. 'We need a plan. Salty, I want you to take 'Er Ladyship back to my 'otel and let Loveday and Tilly look after 'er. I'm goin' back to Crabstock Cove in the punt to link up with Potsy and Dory. We've a fight on our 'ands and there's one or two cats need teachin' a lesson.'

Tilly turned from the guard rail at Sooty's rallying cry. 'Please let me come with you. I owe it to Hettie to see what happened to her, and I want her brought out of there so I can take her home.'

Sooty took one look at Tilly's face and decided not to argue. 'Come on, then – let's get goin'.' He climbed into the punt and Salty lowered Tilly down to join him. When they were clear of the boat, Salty hauled up the anchor and the *Maid of Kelynack* sailed off to safe harbour.

# CHAPTER TWENTY-THREE

The little punt cut through the water at speed as Sooty sculled towards the shore. Both cats leapt from the boat as it beached, and Sooty dragged it up onto the snowy sand. Tilly removed her life jacket and stowed it away in the punt, and Sooty handed her a torch and what looked like a baseball bat. 'I'm not saying you'll need this, but it might come in 'andy if there's a fight.'

Tilly nodded and followed him across the sand into the mouth of the cave, where a small hole had been blown in the iron bars. They made swift progress into the cellars, stopping only briefly at the dresser where Hettie had hidden Lady Crabstock. Tilly moved her torch across the floor. To her horror, there was a trail of blood and several tufts of tabby fur leading to the stone steps up to the kitchen. She knew she was staring at Hettie's blood: it must be Hettie's, because – to her knowledge – ghosts didn't bleed. Based on the gory trail leading to the kitchen, she knew that there was worse to come and forced herself to follow Sooty up the steps.

The kitchen door was ajar and Sooty listened for any sound before pushing it open. The sight before him was one he would never forget, and he tried to save Tilly from it but was too slow. The scene was lit by the flames from the kitchen fire, throwing shadows around the walls that flickered on the carnage before them. Hevva Bunn sat slumped in a chair by the fire, surrounded by empty bottles; his paws and shirt were splattered with blood, which also decorated the wall and the floor by the kitchen table; there, on the tabletop, a number of blood-stained knives glistened in the light of a single candle.

Tilly recognised Christmas Paws before she noticed Hettie. The hag-like creature lay on the floor by the table in a pool of very un-ghostlike blood, her mop cap abandoned by her head, which was so badly beaten that no features remained. The rest of her body was punctuated with a series of deep stab wounds, all adding to the certainty that Christmas Paws had died for a second time.

Hettie sat in the corner of the room on a tall-backed kitchen chair, her head slumped onto her chest. She was bound to the chair by ropes, her legs tied together, and a filthy rag forced into her mouth. Her nose had bled all over her jumper, and Tilly stupidly found herself thinking how cross Hettie would have been to have made such a mess of one of her best business pullovers. Hettie's eyes were closed and swollen; she, too, had been beaten before embracing the merciful oblivion that death offered. Hevva Bunn's belt with its blood-stained buckle lay on the flagstone floor beside her, a brutal reminder of her last moments.

Tilly opened her mouth to scream but no sound would come. Sooty crossed the kitchen to comfort her as the noise of a door slamming came from somewhere in the house. Potsy and Dory had clearly got tired of waiting for Sooty's signal and had entered the manor, but the whirlwind that blew down the kitchen corridor from the main house had very little to do with the vigilante army of Porthladlers.

"Evva Bunn!' came the familiar voice as Tilly fought hard in her grief for recognition. 'You'll suffer for this night's work, and for all the other days of your life.' The figure – dressed from head to toe in a bright red cloak – stopped in her tracks to survey the carnage before lifting Hevva Bunn out of his chair and repeatedly banging his head against the stone fireplace. Pausing briefly to make sure he was conscious, she took a metal fish slice from the range and beat him with it until he cowered for mercy, his paws protecting his bleeding head.

Tilly was rooted to the spot and Sooty could only look on with admiration as Lamorna Tweek continued her assault on her brother. 'You think you're so clever, don't you? Runnin' Crabstock like you belong, blamin' them terrible murders on a ghost. Well, your killin' spree ends 'ere. You've brought shame to our family, an' as for poor Lady Crabstock, I seen 'er just now bein' unloaded down the 'arbour, an' there's more flesh on a bit of cod, you evil piece of nothin'.'

Lamorna allowed her brother to catch his breath, which was a mistake. He suddenly sprang at her, arming himself with one of the knives from the table. Holding her in a vice-like grip, he held the knife to her throat, daring Sooty or Tilly to intervene. 'Just the three of you to finish off and my work is done 'ere,' he said. 'Now my dear little sister, shall I burn you alive in the fireplace or would you prefer a nice stabbin' like my darlin' Saffron 'ere?' He kicked the lifeless form which lay on the floor and Tilly gasped in horror at the realisation that the unrecognisable corpse dressed as Christmas Paws was in fact Saffron Bunn.

Hevva Bunn shot a look at Tilly. 'Yes, I see your penny 'as dropped. Not bad for a so-called detective, but not good enough to save your meddlin' friend 'ere, are you? I made 'er squeal for mercy and enjoyed every minute of it. She took longer than the others to die, although removin' Lord Wingate's eyes while 'e was still breathin' was one of my highlights. Come to think of it, bashin' young Tamsyn's brains out with that pineapple was good fun, too. Fact is, once I'd started I just couldn't stop. Anyway, time is short and I 'ave a boat full of Crabstock valuables moored off the Lizard to attend to, so 'ose goin' first?'

'I think you'll find that you are.' The voice came from the kitchen corridor, distracting Hevva Bunn long enough for Sooty to grab the knife from Lamorna's throat. In one swift movement, Absalom Tweek lifted Bunn off his feet and tossed him through the air like a rag doll. He landed on his head with a resounding crack and lay motionless next to Saffron's body.

'Well done, my luvver,' said Lamorna, watching with satisfaction as a dark lake of blood grew on the flagstones around her brother's head. 'You done for 'im all right, an' not a minute too soon.' Lamorna looked up for the first time since her arrival in the kitchen, and took in the scene of carnage before her. Her eyes came to rest on Hettie's lifeless form, then on the grief-stricken figure of Tilly. 'Oh, my poor dear! I'm so very sorry for your loss, and ashamed that it was at the 'ands of my own brother. Let's get you out of 'ere while Absalom and Sooty sort things out.'

Tilly found her voice and spoke slowly and deliberately. 'I want to take Hettie home to our town, where she can have a proper funeral surrounded by the people who love and respect her. I won't leave without her.'

Lamorna exchanged glances with Sooty and Absalom. 'I'm sure we can 'elp with that. First thing is to make 'er a bit more comfortable for 'er journey.' Lamorna nodded to her husband, who pulled his penknife from his pocket and proceeded to cut the ropes which bound Hettie's body to the chair. He gently pulled the rag from her mouth and cradled her in his arms. One of her wellingtons fell off and Tilly pounced to retrieve it, following Absalom out of the kitchen and down the corridor into the main hall. Lamorna and Sooty joined the sad procession and, on reaching the front door, which was now wide open, they were met by what looked like the entire village of Porthladle, all standing silently in the snow, their flaming torches and lanterns held high. As one, they removed their woolly hats in respect as Absalom bore Hettie's body to the horse and cart which stood waiting in the driveway. 'You sit there a while. Me and Lamorna 'ave a couple of things to sort an' then we'll get you both 'ome.'

Tilly climbed into the back of the cart and sat next to Hettie. Absalom offered a blanket to cover her up, but she refused. She never wanted to be warm again. If Hettie would never feel the joy of a warm fire again, then neither would she. It had begun to snow again, and she watched as the flakes fell from the sky; some settled on Hettie's face and whiskers, and she gently wiped them away. She realised that she'd never truly studied Hettie's face before, and now she marvelled at how perfectly the tabby stripes matched on either side of her face; in spite of her swollen eyes, Hettie Bagshot was a handsome cat. Tilly's tears fell onto her face, mingling with the snowflakes; she didn't notice that the crowd outside the manor house had now moved inside, and only when she heard the crackle of the flames did she lift her head.

Lamorna was first to leave the manor and the smoke followed her out of the door. The rest of the villagers followed swiftly behind her and gathered outside. Tiffy Fluff moved among them, collecting vox pops on her tape recorder, certain that a story like this would give her radio career the boost it deserved. Absalom and Sooty were the last to leave the building; they carried a trunk full of the personal treasures which they had rescued for Lady Crabstock – jewellery, papers and a very saleable collection of gold coins, all gathered in the hope that Her Ladyship would be able to put them to good use in a new life.

All were safely assembled in front of Crabstock Manor, admiring their work as the flames engulfed the house, purifying the evil in which it had bathed for so long. Not even the snow could dampen the boiling inferno that swept through the building. Suddenly, all eyes looked up at the roof and there stood the defiant figure of Hevva Bunn, his clothes burning as his screams added to the cacophony of falling masonry

221

and breaking glass. His body seemed to melt before their eyes like some demon returning to the pit of hell. A roar of approval went up from the villagers as justice was served, and they turned away from the burning building to trudge back across the snow to their own firesides.

Sooty was pleased to see that for once Marlon Brandish and his van had braved the weather, and were well placed to take him and Lady Crabstock-Singe's rescued treasure back to the hotel. On the strength of her best smile, Tiffy Fluff was invited to ride in the back and she clambered eagerly on board, hoping for an exclusive interview with Eloise Crabstock.

But for the body of her best friend lying next to her in Absalom Tweek's cart, Tilly would have been happy to call their Cornish adventure 'case solved', but the No. 2 Feline Detective Agency couldn't have been further from her thoughts as she watched Crabstock Manor burning slowly to the ground.

# CHAPTER TWENTY-FOUR

For those who believe in the magic of Christmas, what happened next should come as no great surprise. Absalom Tweek swung himself up into his driver's seat and offered his paw to Lamorna, who hauled herself up next to him. With a crack of the whip, his horse responded. Wheeling the cart round, they took off down the driveway, cutting through the newly fallen snow until they reached the cliff road. With a sudden pull on the reins, he turned the cart towards the cliff and drove them over the edge.

Caring little for what happened next, Tilly waited for the impact of the cart hitting the rocks below, but it didn't happen. Instead, the Tweeks took flight and climbed high above the sea until the blazing sight of Crabstock Manor was a distant, dull red glow. All

Tilly could remember later was the striking of the Porthladle clock as they passed over the village. It was midnight, and it was Christmas Eve.

'"Good Spirit," he pursued, as down upon the ground he fell before it. "Your nature intercedes for me, and pities me. Assure me that I yet may change these shadows you have shown me, by an altered life!"

'The kind hand trembled.

'"I will honour Christmas in my heart, and try to keep it all year. I will live in the Past, the Present, and the Future. The Spirits of all Three shall strive within me. I will not shut out the lessons that they teach. Oh, tell me I may sponge away the writing on this stone!"'

Tilly sneezed and sat up. Hettie let her copy of *A Christmas Carol* slide to the floor, shocked to see her friend back in the land of the living. The feeling was mutual and the two cats stared at each other, hardly daring to speak in case the moment dissolved into nothing. Their joy was enough to make them both cry out, and they hugged each other tightly, confirming that they were both very much alive.

Hettie was the first to summon up some words. 'You've been so ill. We've all been taking it in turns to sit with you. Look how many books we've got through!' Hettie nodded towards a stack of Tilly's favourite books. 'Nurse Featherstone Clump said we should read to you, even though you were unconscious.

She said it would keep you with us if you could hear our voices.'

Tilly – still not entirely ready to take in anything except the knowledge that Hettie was no longer dead, and that she was at home on her own cushion in front of a warm fire – tried to speak, only to discover that the flu had taken away her voice and replaced it with a high-pitched squeak.

Hettie sprang to the staff sideboard which was covered in various flu remedies, all brought in by their friends over the last few days. There was a home-made cough mixture from Irene Peggledrip; a jar of honey from Jessie at the charity shop; a large bag of wine gums for sucking from Meridian Hambone, who kept the hardware store; a basket of fruit from Malkin and Sprinkle; a small bottle of cod liver oil from Elsie Haddock; and a packet of throat lozenges from Lavender Stamp, who had given Tilly the flu in the first place. She grabbed the lozenges and unwrapped one of them, popping it into Tilly's mouth. The lozenge, like Lavender Stamp herself, was only bearable in small doses and as soon as Tilly felt the full force of its healing qualities she spat it out into the fire. 'Oh! That was disgusting!' she squeaked. 'Even worse than Saffron Bunn's grey porridge.'

'Saffron Bunn?' repeated Hettie. 'Isn't that a Cornish cake?'

'Don't be silly,' squeaked Tilly. 'The Saffron Bunn

who dressed up as Christmas Paws and haunted Crabstock Manor!'

'Saffron Bunn? Christmas Paws? What on earth are you talking about?' asked Hettie, beginning to fear that Tilly was slipping back into the delirious state in which she had been for days.

Tilly didn't answer straight away. Instead, she looked around their room for the first time since waking up, taking in every tiny detail: the filing cabinet where they kept their clothes; Hettie's desk, which doubled as their dining table; the staff sideboard, which contained everything that was useful to them, including the telephone – muffled in old cushions because Hettie hated it to ring and regarded it as a breach of her peace. There were other things in the room that were unfamiliar but no less comforting: a beautifully shaped real Christmas tree, half decorated and clearly a work in progress; a pile of small wrapped presents, stacked neatly in the corner by the TV; and there, in front of her, was Hettie's armchair, with her hastily abandoned dressing gown draped across it.

Her eyes filled with tears as she looked up at Hettie from her cushion. 'I thought you were dead. Hevva Bunn tied you to a chair and tortured you, and if it hadn't been for Lamorna and Absalom Tweek we would never have got home. Don't you remember? You saved Lady Crabstock by hiding her in a Welsh dresser like the one Jessie has in her back room at the charity shop. They all took their hats off to you when Absalom carried your body to the cart.' Tilly's squeaky voice subsided into a bout of uncontrollable sobbing, and all Hettie could do was wait until it had died down.

When the sobs had transformed themselves into the occasional hiccup, Hettie chose her moment to try and make sense of Tilly's anguish. 'I think we could both do with a nice cup of milky tea,' she said brightly. 'And how about something to eat? Anything you like in the whole world.'

Tilly responded with another loud sob. 'I've just remembered! I've left my tartan shopper at Sooty's hotel, and the suitcase with all our best clothes in it. There was no time to pick it up as we flew out of Porthladle in Absalom and Lamorna's cart!'

During the days of illness, Hettie had been very aware that Tilly was as far away as possible from reality. The fever had flared and died as Tilly rambled, twisting and turning in her sleep. There had been waking moments when she sat up and held complete conversations with cats that Hettie had never heard of, and she had put this trance-like state down to the flu that had invaded Tilly's mind and body – but the clarity with which Tilly was now able to recall some of those moments frightened her.

While the kettle boiled, Hettie left their room and returned seconds later, barging the door open

227

with Tilly's tartan shopper. 'There you are,' she said, wheeling it into the room. 'Safe and sound and parked next to the Butters' bread ovens. Now what would you like to eat? I'm starving, so let's have something really nice.'

Tilly's joy at being reunited with her tartan shopper, coupled with the obvious fact that Hettie wasn't dead after all, suddenly perked up her appetite. 'Scrumbled eggs!' she squeaked, 'and lots of buttery toast.'

Hettie was delighted at such a definite response. 'Excellent choice, but don't you mean scrambled?'

Tilly giggled for the first time for days. 'No – scrumbled is the way I want them, with the white bits like Lamorna does them at Jam Makers Inn.'

Hettie ignored any further references to what had now become the secret world of Tilly and added more coal to the fire. 'You drink your tea up and I'll go and see if Betty or Beryl can rustle us up some breakfast. They'll be so pleased you're feeling better.' Hettie left Tilly to her tea and made her way out of the back door and down the alleyway to the front of the Butters' pie and pastry shop.

Tilly stared into the fire, her mind still full of the fantastical journey that she had been on. It was all so very real, and the characters who had glided in and out of what she was now beginning to accept as a very vivid nightmare still seemed to lurk in the back of her mind. She looked at the pile of books that Hettie had pointed to and thought how kind it was of her friends to come and read to her. She had no recollection of their being there, nor any memory of the stories they had chosen, but looking at the titles it was easy to see that they had in a strange sort of way influenced the dream world she had recently inhabited. Mr Dickens' *A Christmas Carol* lay abandoned on the floor by Hettie's armchair; *Jamaica Inn* and *The Hound of the Baskervilles* were balanced precariously on top of the stack by the staff sideboard, along with *Oliver Twist*, Agatha Crispy's *Murder on the Orient Express* and *Ten Little Kittens*; she smiled to see that there was a Poldark novel and several Catrine Cookpot paperbacks which the Butters had obviously brought in to read to her – tales of hardship and brutality, set against the backdrop of the Lancashire mill towns where the sisters had grown up, a world where Hevva Bunn would have felt very much at home, along with Loveday Whisk and even Evergreen Flinch.

As a devourer of books, Tilly understood what it was like to live with a good story long after a particular novel had been returned to Turner Page's library. She was now beginning to understand the continuous theatre that had played out in her mind as she hovered between life and death on her cushion by the fire. But she had to agree with herself, it had been a very good story, a story that she might even write down one day – if she could remember it.

# CHAPTER TWENTY-FIVE

The hot buttered toast and scrumbled eggs arrived with great ceremony as both Betty and Beryl bustled into the room, followed by Hettie and an array of assorted pies and pastries to 'tempt the patient', as Betty had put it.

'Now then, Miss Tilly, you need fattening up, my lass,' said Betty placing a mountain of what would now for ever be known as scrumbled eggs in front of her. 'No more than a pipe cleaner, you are.'

'Ee and you can get yer whiskers round this cream horn when you've finished that,' said Beryl. 'Fresh-baked this morning, just how you like it. You need spoiling, you do. Got to get your strength up for your Christmas dinner tomorrow. There's a nice big turkey and all the trimmings laid on.'

Tilly spluttered on a spoonful of egg that Betty was attempting to post into her mouth. 'You mean today is Christmas Eve?' she squeaked, making everyone laugh.

'Bless you,' said Betty. 'Back with us just in time for Christmas, and the best present any of us could wish for. Poor Hettie's nearly wasted away she's been so worried. Couldn't even tempt her with one of my best sausage pies. She's worn a hole in your carpet, pacing up and down. And as for Bruiser, he's washed that motorbike and sidecar every day, polished it till it gleams ready to take you out for a ride when you got better.'

Beryl nodded to Hettie, encouraging her to get on with her own breakfast, and the two sisters left them in peace to enjoy the treats they had so joyfully given in celebration of Tilly's recovery. The peace didn't last long, as word soon spread that Tilly had rallied. First over the threshold was Bruiser – or, to be precise, the biggest bunch of red carnations followed by Bruiser, who used them to hide his shyness. 'These is from Miss Scarlet and me,' he said, hopping from one paw to another. 'They're a bit Christmassy and that'll brighten up yer sideboard. Meridian Hambone let me 'ave 'em 'alf price as they were fer you. Miss Scarlet's all lovely and shiny and waitin' till you're well enough fer a little spin out.'

Tilly beamed at the thought of a trip in Miss Scarlet. The image of Marlon Brandish and his beaten-up old van popped into her head, but she knew now that he was a figment of her imagination and graciously accepted the flowers. Bruiser, thrilled to see Tilly looking so much better, skipped down the garden path back to his shed to carry on reading the Christmas edition of *Biker's Monthly* in the company of Miss Scarlet and his paraffin stove.

Hettie put the carnations in a jam jar on the staff sideboard and took in their room for the first time in days, realising that – quite simply – it resembled a pigsty. The table was full of half-eaten plates of food; there were several mugs of untouched beef tea, boxes of tissues, and clothes strewn everywhere; and in the middle of it all a half-hearted attempt at Christmas. The tree was beautiful, but strangely out of place amid the chaos.

Tilly had made a good effort with her scrumbled eggs, although the front of her pyjamas had also benefited from her breakfast. Hettie cleared away the dishes, piling them up in the small sink which was already overflowing with dirty crockery. She had never regarded cleaning as a priority, and only since Tilly moved in had she felt the benefit of a clean and tidy home. Tilly was undoubtedly the home-maker, and without her, even after just a few days, things had got out of hand. Hettie sighed as she stared at the mountain of washing-up, not really knowing where to start, but help was about to knock on the back door.

Tilly's friend Jessie ran the charity shop in Cheapcuts

Lane. She'd inherited the shop from Miss Lambert, an elderly cat who adopted Jessie after she was abandoned as a kitten. Jessie had become a permanent fixture in Miss Lambert's life and she had nursed her in her final months. In the days when Tilly had wandered the streets of the town, cold and hungry, Miss Lambert had occasionally taken her in and given her a warm bed and a hot meal, and that was how Tilly and Jessie had become friends. These days, Tilly was often called upon to mind the shop for the odd afternoon, which gave her an excellent opportunity to choose from Jessie's extensive cardigan range, kept in stock especially for her.

Jessie had spent many hours reading to Tilly over the last few days, allowing Hettie to take the occasional brief nap or stock up with shopping. She had been desperately worried about her friend, and had decided to shut her shop on Christmas Eve to spend more time with her. The last thing she had expected to see was Tilly sitting up on her cushion, beaming as she bustled into the room laden with Christmas parcels. 'Well, aren't you a sight for sore eyes?' she said, dropping her parcels on the floor and bounding over to give Tilly a hug. Taking off the red cloche hat that she always wore, Jessie looked for somewhere to put it and realised that the best place was back on her head. 'You two look like you could benefit from a bit of a bottoming, as Miss Lambert used to say. Shall I roll my sleeves up and get stuck in?'

It was Hettie's turn to smile. 'That would be lovely if you can spare the time. I'm afraid I've let things go a bit.'

'That's probably the understatement of the week,' said Jessie. 'But running a hospital wing isn't the easiest thing to do and you've managed brilliantly. Look – your patient is doing very well. Why don't you make us all a nice cup of tea and I'll have this mess sorted out in no time.'

Hettie tackled the washing-up with a new resolve as Jessie set about the room like a whirling dervish. Within a very short space of time, all was spick and span.

'I'd quite like to get dressed,' squeaked Tilly, throwing her blanket off. 'These pyjamas don't look very nice.'

Jessie reached for one of the parcels she'd brought with her. 'As you're feeling better you can have an early present.'

Tilly took the parcel and tore the paper off to reveal a bright red cardigan, decorated with white snowflakes, patch pockets and a hood. 'Ooh that's the loveliest cardigan I've ever seen, and I can wear it with my best green woolly socks!'

Hettie and Jessie laughed as Tilly threw off her pyjamas and wriggled into her Christmas cardigan. It fitted perfectly, and Tilly was so pleased with it that she would wear it constantly until the early summer heat forced her to abandon it. Jessie stayed for a while, exchanging bits of the town's gossip as the three cats munched through a selection of mince pies and sausage rolls from the Butters' tray of treats. Tilly was growing stronger by the minute, and Hettie noted that if her appetite was anything to go by, she was well and truly on the mend.

When Jessie had gone, Hettie filled up the coal scuttle from the stack in the Butters' backyard. She suddenly felt so very tired, and for the first time she realised that she had hardly slept since Tilly had been taken ill. Her days and nights had blended into one, punctuated only by visits from friends and well-wishers. She struggled back in with the coal scuttle to find Tilly adding baubles to the half-dressed Christmas tree.

'Don't overdo it,' she said. 'You should have a rest. You've had a very busy morning and we want you at your best for Christmas day upstairs at the Butters'.'

Tilly clapped her paws in excitement. 'I think it's going to be the best Christmas ever! Why don't you have a sleep while I finish the tree?'

Hettie crawled into her armchair and immediately fell asleep to the contented sound of Tilly squeaking her way through a selection of Christmas carols.

# CHAPTER TWENTY-SIX

Hettie awoke with a start several hours later. She hadn't meant to fall into such a deep sleep but the relief she felt on opening her eyes to find Tilly sitting on her cushion, working her way through a pile of Christmas cards, made her heart sing.

'Ooh good,' said Tilly. 'If you're awake we can have the TV on. It's time for *Carols from King's*. I know you think the nine lessons are boring, but those tiny kitten choristers are lovely to watch. And look – I've opened all our Christmas cards and there are some shiny, sparkly ones. There's also something addressed to the No. 2 Feline Detective Agency, but I haven't bothered with that as it's Christmas.'

Hettie stretched, noticing that Tilly and her new Christmas cardigan were covered in bits of glitter, and she glistened like one of the many cards in front of her. 'You look like something you've forgotten to hang on the tree,' she said, laughing as Tilly switched on the TV just in time to watch a lone kitten strike up the first verse of 'Once in Royal David's City'. The carol service was embraced by cats all over the world, and even Hettie – who thought that the religious aspect of Christmas spoilt the rest of it – had to admit that the sight of a choir of tiny kittens dressed in white was enough to bring a tear to the eye of even the most extreme atheist.

Wiping that particular tear away, she flung off her blanket and devoted some time to making herself a little more presentable. The cleaning ritual required more effort than usual, as she had to chew out several stubborn tangles which had gathered in her long tabby fur when she wasn't looking; during the dark days of Tilly's illness, it wasn't just their room that she had neglected. Satisfied that her appearance was greatly improved, she selected a bright red jumper and a clean pair of 'at home' slacks from the filing cabinet.

Tilly sat glued to the pomp and ceremony of Christmas, occasionally adding her squeaky voice to the carols she liked best. In her mind, she found herself revisiting the terrifying blizzard as she escaped from Crabstock Manor, and she wondered why the delirium brought about by her cat flu was having such a profound effect on her. She wanted to share what had been a very strange adventure with Hettie, but the horrific turn of events was too fresh in her mind to speak it out loud. Here, in their safe, secure world, there was no room for anything that would spoil Christmas.

Hettie busied herself in putting the mountain of cards up around their room. By the time she had finished, the staff sideboard looked considerably more festive than it had earlier and the mantelpiece – reserved for sparkly cards only – looked a picture. With great relief, she recognised the opening notes of 'Hark! The Herald Angels Sing', and with the end of the carol service in sight, she felt able to raise the subject of supper. 'How about fish and chips for tea?' she suggested. 'I could pop down to Elsie Haddock's and pick some up as a treat. It is Christmas Eve, after all.'

Tilly clapped her paws together in sheer delight, pushing a vision of Arnold Fritter to the back of her mind. 'That would be lovely! Shall I find us something nice on TV to go with them?' She picked up the copy of the *Daily Snout* which lay discarded by Hettie's chair and boasted a full run-down of radio and television for the holidays. Although it was the Christmas edition of the town's daily newspaper, there was very little cheer on the front page: the headline proclaimed 'DEATH TOLL REACHES 100', and Tilly fell silent as she read the article, knowing how close she had been to becoming a cat flu statistic.

Hettie buttered several slices of bread, knowing that they would need a chip butty or two with their supper. 'Shall we have fiery ginger beer or a cup of tea?'

Tilly thought for a moment as she flicked through the TV listings. 'I think ginger beer might be too scratchy for my throat, so a cup of tea would be nice. Oh that's good – *It's a Wonderful Cat* is on at seven, followed by *Scrooge on Ice*.'

Hettie cringed at Tilly's selection, hoping that the catnip she intended to smoke later would dilute the sentimental nonsense in which her friend invested so much viewing time. 'Does it get better later?' she asked. Tilly gasped as she read that Hitchcock's *Jamaica Inn* had been programmed for the midnight movie slot, and Hettie looked at her, puzzled. 'Why are you upset? It's one of your favourite films, and you love the book. I read you most of it while you were ill.'

Tilly sidestepped the question as images of Absalom and Lamorna Tweek knocked on her psyche. 'I think a midnight movie might be a bit late for me, especially as we have such a busy day tomorrow.'

The realisation that she had made no proper preparations for Christmas day suddenly put Hettie into a panic. According to the clock on the staff sideboard, it was half past four on Christmas Eve and she hadn't wrapped so much as one present for Tilly. In all honesty, she hadn't had the heart even to think about Christmas while her friend was lying so gravely ill, and now she had nothing to give her. 'I think I'll have to pop out for a bit,' she said, as nonchalantly as she could. 'There are a couple of things I need to attend to before I pick up the fish and chips. Will you be OK or shall I ask Bruiser to come and sit with you?'

Tilly was still deeply engrossed in the TV pages and suddenly squealed with delight. 'Look! *Cleopatra*'s starting any minute! What a treat!' She scrambled to change the channel and was just in time to see the opening titles proclaim that her favourite actress, Elizabeth Traybake, was about to lead a cast of thousands in a two-and-a-half-hour epic of Roman intrigue. Hettie piled more coal on the fire, grabbed her coat, scarf and hat and a ten-pound note from her desk drawer, and left Tilly engrossed, praying as she trudged out into the cold that some shops in the high street would still be open for last-minute purchases.

As she came down the alleyway, she noticed that Lavender Stamp's post office was shut. The Butters had long since wiped their surfaces down in the bakery, and there was no sign of life at Hilda Dabit's dry cleaners. With great relief, she noticed that Elsie Haddock's Fish Emporium was in full swing and she quickened her step towards Hambone's hardware store, hoping that Meridian might have lingered in order to catch a late pound or two before the lure of a festive bottle of milk stout got the better of her. She was in luck:

the pavement at the front of the shop boasted a few bedraggled Christmas trees and a couple of poinsettias which were desperate for a drink, and the lights were on inside. Pleased that she wasn't too late to buy Tilly something nice, Hettie wasted no time in pushing the door open.

'Blimey! If it ain't Sherlock 'erself,' came the greeting from Meridian Hambone as she sat perched behind her counter, her long claws grappling with a pair of knitting needles which were creating something woolly and yellow. 'I was just about to call it a day. You lookin' for anything special?'

'Yes, I need some presents for Tilly,' Hettie replied, trying not to sound too desperate.

'Well yer's come to the right place, then, 'aven't yer? She must be past 'er flu if yer getting presents. That's a nice bit of news. What sort of stuff are yer lookin' for? I got some nice bits in me 'lectrics department, and they make nice Christmas boxes. You go an 'ave a good look.'

Hettie made her way to the bottom of the shop, picking up a trolley on the way. She passed an Aladdin's cave of homeware, garden tools, paint, and a particularly large display of patterned Fablon sticky-backed plastic which Meridian's son, Lazarus, had come by. Lazarus had an eye for things that fell off the back of lorries, and he made sure that his mother's shop was first to benefit. Hettie smiled as she

241

passed the Fablon, remembering how Betty and Beryl Butter had come to Lavender Stamp's rescue back in the summer; on the hottest day of the year, Lavender had decided to give her kitchen surfaces a makeover, but had bonded with the Fablon herself long before it reached her units; the Butters had used up a whole tin of Vim cleaner in scrubbing the sticky mess off the embarrassed post mistress.

Meridian Hambone's electrical department was one of the most popular outlets in the town, partly due to her prices and partly to the innovative range of stock. The latest fashions and trends could always be found, often minus their boxes and occasionally with the added bonus of a dent or two which kept the ticket price modest and the turnover brisk. Lazarus, thanks to his dubious contacts, had filled the shelves with interesting gadgets, and Hettie could have hugged him for it. The Teasmade was the first item to catch her eye, complete with two mugs and a built-in radio clock alarm; it would be just right for those cold mornings when Tilly had to struggle off her cushion to make their tea. On the shelf below the Teasmade was a bundle of pink electric blankets. Hettie pulled one out to take a closer look, debating in her head whether a hot-water bottle might be more comforting, but as Tilly had several hot-water bottles already, she decided to go for broke and selected the electric blanket that had the least amount of water staining on it. She noticed that there was a shelf of colourful alarm clocks just past the electrical section and settled for a shiny silver one with a vintage motorbike on its face – that would be perfect for Bruiser, as his getting up in the morning was a bit hit-and-miss.

Satisfied with her choices so far, Hettie moved back down the shop, stopping at the stationery fixture to select a couple of rolls of wrapping paper to add to her trolley. She still needed a gift for the Butters – without them, life would have been unbearable these last few days, and she would be forever grateful to them for the home that she and Tilly shared. She knew that they loved their garden, but the problem was knowing what to buy for it. She stared at the bewildering array of garden tools, lawnmowers, pots and assorted plastic gnomes, then – out of the corner of her eye – she spied exactly the right thing: a do-it-yourself garden bench, still in its box and ready to be wrapped. She pounced on it and hauled it into the trolley, then made her way back down the aisle to the counter.

'Gawd love us!' squawked Meridian. 'You 'ave been busy. Let's 'ave a look – paper's on discount, 'lectric blanket's in me sale, Teasmade you can 'ave fer a fiver. What say the lot fer a tenner as it's Christmas?'

Hettie beamed as she handed the money over. 'I don't suppose I could borrow the trolley to get it all home?' she asked, pushing her luck.

Meridian sighed. 'You don't want much, do yer?

Doin' a poor old cat over at this time on a Christmas Eve, an' then askin' for transport! You'll be expectin' me to wrap the stuff next.' Meridian cackled at the look on Hettie's face. 'Go on with yer! I was only 'avin' a little joke. Bring me trolley back in the New Year. I'm shuttin' up till then.'

Hettie boomed out her 'Merry Christmas' as she left Hambone's behind and made her way back up the high street, crossing the road to join the queue outside Elsie Haddock's. It was a jolly crowd, all waiting in anticipation for the prize of a newspaper parcel of golden battered fish and hot chips, fried to perfection by Elsie's own large paws. Hettie waited patiently with her trolley as the queue moved into the shop; not wishing to leave it outside, she took it in with her, much to the annoyance of a grossly overweight cat who was trying to get out. For a moment or two, tempers flared as she became wedged between Hettie's trolley and the door, offering several words that Hettie would only ever say under her breath, but at last the fat cat spilt out into the street and the festive spirit returned.

There was only one cat left in front of her when Hettie realised that she had spent all her money in Hambone's and had nothing left to pay for the tea with. She felt the hot, red stain of embarrassment rise to the top of her ears and looked round shiftily for anyone she recognised in the queue who might sub her out of trouble, but there was no one from whom she felt she could borrow. Her turn came and she stared blankly at Elsie, who stood wielding a wire basket full of freshly fried chips. 'I've only got the cod now,' she said apologetically. 'Haddock's all gone. Is that fish and chips twice?' Hettie nodded as Elsie slapped two sizzling pieces of battered cod and two large shovels of chips in newspaper and handed them over the counter. She fumbled in her empty pockets but Elsie raised her paw. 'Put your money away! Have these on me in celebration of Miss Tilly's recovery. Jessie was in earlier and told me she was better. Happy Christmas to you both!'

Scarcely believing her luck, Hettie added the parcel of fish and chips to her trolley, returned Elsie's Christmas wishes to her and the rest of the queue, and headed home as the snow began to fall.

# CHAPTER TWENTY-SEVEN

It was only a short distance home, but the snow was settling fast. By the time that Hettie had reached the Butters' shop, there was a thick covering on the ground and the wheels of Meridian Hambone's trolley had developed a spirit of resistance to moving forward, let alone in a straight line. Hettie virtually carried the trolley for the last few yards, and parked the offending item by one of the bread ovens at the back door.

Tilly hardly noticed that she had returned, as Cleopatra was preparing to play out her final death scene with Mark Antony in her pyramid. Not wishing to disturb her, Hettie grabbed the Sellotape from her desk drawer and went to do battle with the Christmas paper and the contents of the trolley. The fish and chips were still warm, in spite of the snowstorm they'd been subjected to, and Hettie unloaded them into one of the ovens which still held the heat from the Butters' final batch of pies. Wrapping anything had never been high on her list of achievements; her large paws always seemed to get in the way of any careful folding, and the end of the Sellotape was a mystery that had to be solved every time she reached for it. Eventually, she managed to make a reasonable job of Tilly's and Bruiser's presents, but the bench proved too much for her and she decided that she would need Tilly's assistance with such a big box. She put the wrapped presents back in the trolley and dragged the big box and what was left of the wrapping paper into their room, only to find Tilly sobbing her heart out.

'Whatever's happened? Are you feeling ill again?'

Tilly looked up, her eyes full of tears. 'No, I'm all right, but I wish there was a happy ending for Elizabeth Traybake. She always dies and in such a nasty way, bitten by an asp viper and bricked up in a pyramid. I wish I hadn't watched it now.'

Hettie worked hard to resist the laughter that rose in her throat. 'I'm sure that the *actual* Elizabeth Traybake is having a lovely Christmas, just like we are. As for Cleopatra, it was all so long ago that I'm sure she's stopped minding being bricked up in a pyramid. Anyway, it's time for our fish and chips, and I've got something exciting to show you out of the window.'

Tilly brightened immediately, wiped her eyes and

247

nose on the sleeve of her Christmas cardigan, and joined Hettie at the window. The snow lay thick in the Butters' backyard and the garden beyond was a real winter wonderland, lightening a night sky which was now full of stars. Hettie expected a squeal of delight from Tilly, who loved the snow; instead she just stared out of the window, pulling her cardigan closer around her. When she eventually spoke, it was in a very far-off voice. 'That big bright one is the North Star. It leads the sailors home.'

Hettie was confused. 'I didn't mean the stars. What about the snow? How perfect is that for Christmas Eve?'

Tilly shivered as the memory of her fall down the mineshaft at Jam Makers Inn came flooding back to her. 'I hope Osbert Twigg is all right. He looked so jolly in Absalom's hat,' she said, returning to the fire to warm her paws.

Hettie shook her head with concern. Tilly was most certainly back in the land of the living, but the cat flu had taken its toll and she was still in a very vulnerable state of mind. 'Look!' she said. 'I've bought a present for us to give to Betty and Beryl. It was a real bargain at Hambone's. I think they'll love it.'

Tilly left the fire to investigate the box that Hettie had propped up by the table. 'That's a lovely present, but it doesn't look very Christmassy.'

Hettie proffered the Christmas paper. 'I thought you

might like to help me wrap it before we have our tea.'

Tilly was thrilled to be involved in wrapping such a big present and cheered up immediately. The two cats battled with paper and Sellotape until the parcel looked almost respectable. They ran out of paper before they'd quite finished, but Tilly improvised and patched the ends with some bits of birthday wrap which she'd stored in the staff sideboard for emergencies.

'Right,' said Hettie, 'I'll stick this out by the ovens and bring in our tea. Let's settle down by the fire and watch the programmes you've chosen for us.' She dragged the box out of the room and returned with the parcel of fish and chips. 'Elsie Haddock has sent these as a present to celebrate your recovery, so you'd better eat them all up.'

Hettie unwrapped the food, dividing it between two plates and filling their room with a tantalising aroma. Tilly purred as the smell reached her nostrils. She suddenly realised how very hungry she was, and the thought of a chip buttery – as she called it – was almost too exciting. The friends sat together in front of the fire, crunching and munching on their supper and watching *It's a Wonderful Cat*. By the time they'd finished, they were both covered in butter and chip fat and had to spend much of the film in a concentrated bout of face, whiskers and ear cleaning. Full and content, Hettie climbed into her armchair and filled her pipe with catnip. Tilly selected an almost clean pair of pyjamas from the filing cabinet and changed out of her Christmas cardigan, settling down on her cushion just as the band struck up the theme to *Scrooge on Ice*.

Tilly loved to watch ice skating and was a big fan of Torpid and Jean, who had taken the international stage by storm with their Ravel's 'Boléro' routine. Torpid was playing Scrooge in this particular Christmas special, and as far as Tilly could see, all the other leading parts in the story were being played by Jean, whose costume changes were a critical part of the performance. Hettie had never seen the point of skating on ice, even though it had become a metaphorical factor in her own life, but she had to admit that – after a pipe of catnip – Torpid and Jean's endeavours looked altogether more entertaining than she had expected. Tilly was mesmerised until the moment when Jean glided across the ice as the Ghost of Christmas Past; at this point, she suddenly lost interest and busied herself in putting some of the presents she'd wrapped under the tree.

Watching her friend turn away from the television at such a high point in the production saddened Hettie, and she knew that she had to encourage Tilly to face up to the demons which were troubling her. 'Come and sit by the fire,' she said. 'I've so missed your chatter since you've been ill, and I think it's time you told me where you've been these last few days.'

Tilly stood back to admire their tree, then returned to her cushion by the fire. 'I'm not sure where to start, really,' she began. 'I'm feeling a bit silly about it all. I know none of it happened, but it still seems so real.'

Hettie refilled her pipe and sat back in her chair as Tilly began her extraordinary story. The characters were so vividly presented that within no time she found herself believing in them as much as Tilly did. It was long past midnight before the story was brought to its horrific conclusion, and Hettie found herself on the edge of her seat as Tilly played out the final acts of her nightmare. When the story was over, the two cats stared into the fire in silent contemplation.

Hettie spoke first. 'No wonder you were so troubled, with all those characters swimming round in your head. I'm surprised you got better at all, but it was certainly an adventure. I just wish I could have been there, instead of filling hot-water bottles, spooning in cough mixture and pacing the floor.'

'But that's the point,' said Tilly. 'You were there. We shared everything, even the nasty bits, like we always do.'

Hettie nodded. 'Well, at least we got a "case solved" out of it. Time for bed, I think. We have a busy day tomorrow.'

'Today,' corrected Tilly. 'Happy Christmas!'

# CHAPTER TWENTY-EIGHT

Hettie woke first, which was a very rare thing. She stretched, strangely happy to embrace the new day without any reservations. The fire was almost out and the clock peeping from between the Christmas cards on the staff sideboard informed her that it was ten past ten: Christmas day was already well established. She gathered some bits of kindling and coaxed the fire into producing tiny flames, adding small bits of coal until the grate came back to life. Tilly slept on, oblivious to the movement around her, and Hettie cast her eye across the tray of pastries that the Butters had left them with the day before. She selected some sausage rolls and a collection of cheese straws and put them onto a plate before switching the kettle on and preparing two mugs for morning tea. Then she pulled the curtains open onto a beautiful, sunlit scene of undisturbed snow, stretching down the Butters' garden to Bruiser's shed at the bottom. Tilly was right. It was the best Christmas ever.

Taking the tea and breakfast back to the fire, she added the greasy newspaper from their supper to the flames, which spat and leapt up the chimney. The crackle woke Tilly, and Hettie added more coal to the flames. 'Ooh, what a lovely sleep I've had,' Tilly said, sitting up. 'And festive pastries for breakfast!' She helped herself to a cheese straw and waved the pastry at Hettie, who had already managed two sausage rolls. 'Better not have too many of these. I think the Butters' Christmas dinner is going to be huge.'

Hettie was pleased to see Tilly looking so bright and untroubled. The burden of her nightmare had been lifted in its telling, and now a day of friends, feasting and a few wrapped surprises stretched out before them. Hettie posted two more sausage rolls into her mouth, brushed the excess pastry which clung to her dressing gown into the fireplace, and headed out into the corridor to fetch one of Tilly's presents.

Betty Butter was staring into the bread ovens and jumped when she realised that Hettie was standing next to her. 'Ee lass, you've frightened me to death, creeping up like that! Me and this 'ere turkey was 'avin' a chat.' She nodded towards the glass door, and there – sizzling in all its glory – was the biggest turkey that Hettie had ever seen. ''E's been in there a good three hours, and 'appen another two will suffice. We don't want tough old drumsticks or dried up breast, do we?'

Hettie marvelled at the sheer size of the bird and secretly wondered how long it would take to carve the creature. No doubt turkey pie would feature highly on the Butters' menu board when they reopened their shop after the holiday. 'Is there anything we can do to help with the lunch?' Hettie asked, keeping her paws crossed that her assistance wouldn't be required.

'Bless you for askin', but sister and I have it all under control. All you need to do is bring yourselves upstairs by one o'clock, both wearin' your eatin' trousers.' Betty made her way back upstairs and Hettie grabbed the wrapped Teasmade. She skipped into their room, pursued by the unmistakable smell of turkey, which added to the festive spirit that positively bounced off the walls.

'You've got two presents from me, one now and one later,' she said, placing the box in front of Tilly.

Tilly clapped her paws with excitement and scrambled under the Christmas tree, emerging with a small parcel. 'And this one's for you!'

Hettie took delivery of the present and Tilly wasted no time in ripping the paper off her own box. She stared at the picture on the front for some time, trying to work out what exactly it was for. 'Aren't you going to get it out of the box?' Hettie prompted.

'It all looks a bit important,' said Tilly earnestly. 'It says it's a two-cup Teasmade, but the picture has a clock face on it.'

'That's because it has a radio clock alarm and it makes the tea!'

Tilly stared in amazement at her present. She was slow to trust new technology and had only just got used to their kettle switching itself off; the thought of a machine that woke you up, switched the radio on and made the tea was almost too much to cope with. Hettie hurried things along by helping her to unpack it, and the two cats set the Teasmade up on the staff sideboard, making sure that the plug reached the socket. Tilly pulled out the instruction leaflet and sat staring at it. 'Gobbledy gook!' she exclaimed, before casting the piece of paper aside. 'Why those Chinese cats think we can all speak Chinese I don't know! And why can't they write across the page instead of up and down?'

Hettie picked up the instructions and had to admit that her Chinese wasn't any better than Tilly's – but there *was* a series of diagrams showing a cat's paw performing various manoeuvres, numbered one to six. 'Let's have a go at this,' she said. 'I'll tell you what to do step by step.'

Tilly stood nervously next to the Teasmade, awaiting Hettie's directions. 'One, plug it in and switch it on.'

Tilly did as she was told and a small red light appeared on the front of the machine, confirming that it was working. 'Two, lift that flap on the top and fill it with water.'

Tilly lifted the flap to tip the water in, only to discover a small packet of tea bags. 'Oh look, we've got extras – good job I saw them before the water went in. What's next?'

'To be honest it's hard to say,' said Hettie, scratching her head. 'I think you've got to set the clock. The knobs are round the back, so you'll have to twiddle them all until we get the right one.' Tilly pushed and pulled on the various controls until the hour and minute hand sprang into life. She set the clock to match the one next to it on the staff sideboard, and awaited further orders. 'The next bit's easy – put a tea bag, milk and sugar into the cups, stick them back into the machine and press that big button on the top.' Tilly did as she was told and stood back, waiting for the magic to begin. The Teasmade stared back at them in defiance. The red light was still visible, the hands on the clock were moving steadily around the face, but they were no closer to having a cup of tea than if they'd ordered it from Malkin and Sprinkle's cafe.

'We may as well put the bloody kettle on,' said Hettie, taking a closer look at the offending item. 'This was too much to hope for, I suppose.' Her words were snatched away by a whirring noise, coming from the

Teasmade; next came a whistling and spitting sound, followed by a full convulsion of boiling water spilling into the cups that Tilly had prepared. The alarm and the radio came on at the same moment, both at full volume, and the overexcited Teasmade danced across the staff sideboard in triumph.

Tilly hid behind Hettie's armchair, thinking that a safe distance was the way to go. Hettie waited until the machine had settled and pounced on the plug socket, switching the machine off and rescuing the two cups of tea it had produced. 'I'm sure we'll get the hang of it eventually,' she said, passing the tea to Tilly.

Surprisingly, the tea was very good and Tilly was thrilled with her present, if not a little alarmed by its behaviour during its inaugural flight. 'I think you should open your present now,' she said, returning to her cushion by the fire. 'It's not as exciting as mine, but I think you'll like it.'

Hettie picked up her present and turned it round in her paws. She sniffed it and finally tore the paper off to reveal a beautifully crafted wooden pipe and a packet of her favourite extra strong catnip. 'What a perfect present! Where did you find such a lovely pipe?'

'I bought it from a stall at the cloche hat and feather festival that Jessie took me to in November. An old cat sat there carving the pipes all day. Look – he's put your initials on it.'

Hettie was very pleased to see 'H. B.' just inside the bowl. It was a very special present and she put it in pride of place on the mantelpiece next to the catnip, hoping that there would be time to try it out when they returned from the Butters' later.

The two cats busied themselves tidying their room and dressing for Christmas lunch. Tilly had decided to wear her new Christmas cardigan, and Hettie picked out a shirt and waistcoat, choosing a pair of her stretch business slacks in the knowledge that Christmas lunch would put a great deal of strain on her waistband. It was five minutes to one, and time to collect the Butters' present and follow the overwhelming smell of turkey up the stairs to their landladies' flat.

# CHAPTER TWENTY-NINE

The door was wide open and Beryl had stationed herself just inside to collect coats and hand out small schooners of sherry. Hettie accepted a sherry, although she wasn't keen – the taste reminded her of a posh sherry party back in the mists of her time which had rendered her speechless and legless for several days. She decided that to refuse would cause offence, though, especially as Tilly had already made it clear to Beryl that she would prefer a Vimto with a straw.

No sooner had Tilly received her Vimto than Lavender Stamp bustled up the stairs looking like something from *The Heroes of Telemark* – or Eskimo Nell, as Hettie would suggest later. She had obviously dressed for the snowy conditions, but the fact that she had only had to cross the road from her post office suggested that her efforts with outdoor clothing were slightly over the top. She eagerly accepted a schooner, and downed it in one before removing her galoshes.

Bruiser came next and had made a real effort: he'd slicked down his hair, combed his unruly whiskers, and sported a rather jaunty striped bow tie which stood out from his ill-fitting jacket and trousers. He carried several small bottles of Babycham, which he exchanged with Beryl for an extra-large sherry.

'Make theeselves at 'ome!' boomed Betty from the door of her kitchenette, looking hot and flustered as she wrestled with the turkey. Having almost completed her task as meeter and greeter, Beryl left one schooner of sherry on the tray and crossed to the record player, where she selected a raucous medley of Christmas favourites performed by Tijuana Brass. Lavender Stamp began to sway in time to an abortive rendering of 'Away in a Manger', and Jessie burst through the door, full of apologies for being late. She'd spent the morning helping the town's librarian, Turner Page, prepare Christmas lunch for local homeless cats. The lunch was being held in Turner's new library and he was expecting quite a crowd, as word had got out that – as well as the food – Turner himself would be performing a selection of favourite readings from Mr Dickens, dressed in his best smoking jacket.

'Take your places!' invited Betty as she staggered

through from the kitchen under the weight of the turkey. 'Bruiser – if you'd like to work your magic with the carving knife, lad, sister and I will follow up with the roasties while they're nice and hot.'

The Butters' table had been extended to seat all their guests and took up most of their dining-room-cum-lounge. The sofa and armchairs had been pushed back against the walls, but the room still maintained an air of sumptuous comfort. The sisters had done well for themselves: their hard work as the town's bakers had paid off, and the flat above their shop – although small – was peppered with the best of everything; uncluttered, tasteful and expensive.

The Christmas table was a work of art, laid out with matching place settings themed in red and silver; there were crackers to match and a beautiful table centre of holly and ivy, punctuated with tiny red glass baubles and three red twisted candles. The glasses were of crystal and shone in the glow of the open fire, which threw ever-shifting patterns across the pure white tablecloth.

Bruiser, as the only male cat in the party, assumed his place at the head of the table with Betty and Beryl on either side of him. The three worked in tandem, loading the plates and passing them down the table. When each plate had been piled so high that nothing else would fit, Beryl removed the substantial remains of the turkey and returned from the kitchen with a gigantic jug of steaming gravy. 'That should wet yer

Yorkshires nicely,' she said, passing the jug to Tilly, who filled the two Yorkshire puddings on her plate and passed the jug to Lavender Stamp, who did the same but succeeded in splashing the tablecloth as well.

Before the assembled company could lift their knives and forks, Betty rose from her seat, nodding to Bruiser who had exchanged his carving knife for a bottle of champagne. He popped the cork on her instruction, making everyone jump, and flew round the table filling glasses. Betty raised her glass. 'Let's drink to all those less fortunate than us, and hope for good health and happiness. And I'd just like to say how very pleased sister and I are to see Miss Tilly back to her old self again. Happy Christmas to us all!'

The clink of crystal filled the room as the friends echoed Betty's sentiments. From that moment on, food and drink fuelled the merriment around the table as they chewed and crunched their way through the mountain of dinner, all topped off with a flaming Christmas pudding that swam in Beryl's best brandy. With the exception of Tilly, who had wisely stuck to Vimto, the rest of the party was more than a little worse for drink by the time they came to dismantle the table to make room for after-dinner activities. Lavender Stamp had actually fallen asleep in her Christmas pudding, but Hettie had woken her with a well-aimed nudge in the ribs. She would have preferred to give the post mistress a slap for the bucketload of disapproval which she'd had to endure throughout the year, but there was no place for violence at such a jolly gathering.

Returning the table to a manageable size proved to be a complicated business, especially when all seven cats insisted on helping. At one point, Betty became trapped in the mechanism, and but for Bruiser's courageous intervention she might have spent Boxing Day nursing a broken paw. There was no doubt that drink had been a major factor in the difficulties, but eventually the table was despatched to its usual place by the window, and the sofa and chairs were brought forward and placed in a semicircle around the fire.

Foolishly, Beryl replenished the glasses as her sister turned on the television just in time to hear the national anthem being put through its paces. Her Majesty loomed into view, ready to address the nation, and the seven cats watched in silence as the Queen praised her subjects and shared some family cinefilm of her own kittens pursuing various worthy tasks during the year. The common theme of her Christmas message was temporarily lost when Lavender Stamp reached for one of Betty's willow pattern vases to relieve herself of the Christmas pudding that had proved a spoonful too far. In spite of the disgusting nature of Lavender's overindulgence, Hettie, Tilly and Jessie shook with laughter as Betty recovered the vase and took it through to the kitchen to rinse it out. Lavender recovered herself and celebrated by downing another glass of champagne before the Queen had been toasted.

Small presents were exchanged as the cats relaxed. Betty and Beryl had bought matching pyjamas for Hettie and Tilly in blue and white stripes with their initials on the pockets, and a pair of leather motorbike gauntlets for Bruiser. Lavender, sparing no expense, had bought pen and propelling pencil sets for everyone, partly due to her generous post office discount but mostly because she had over-ordered for the shop and needed to unload her surplus stock. Jessie bestowed matching scarf and mitten sets on the Butters and a very fine red waistcoat on Bruiser, who flung off his jacket and paraded his present for all to admire, pulling on his new biker gloves to add the finishing touch.

Hettie pulled herself up from the sofa where she'd collapsed after her lunch and dragged the large parcel she'd parked on the landing into the room. 'This one's for Betty and Beryl,' she said, pushing the parcel towards them. 'With love from Tilly, Bruiser and me.'

'Well just look at that, sister!' said Beryl, hauling herself out of her armchair. 'Whatever can it be?'

Betty wasted no time in ripping the paper off and the Butters clapped their paws in sheer delight when they realised that it was a garden bench. 'Ee, fancy that,' said Beryl, pulling the various bits of wood out

of the box. 'I was only saying to sister the other day –
we need a bench for contemplation.'

Hettie and Bruiser sprang to her assistance as the
last few planks of wood were emptied out onto the
carpet. 'Would you like us to put it together?' asked
Bruiser, trying to make sense of the paper diagram that
had fallen out of the box.

'Ee that'd be grand. It could live by the ovens
downstairs next to Tilly's shopper till the spring
comes, and we can sit on it while we're waiting on the
batches, sister.'

Betty nodded in agreement, and – with the
exception of Lavender Stamp, who appeared to have
passed out – all the cats set to building the garden
bench, treating it as a giant communal jigsaw.
Bruiser was the self-appointed foreman, and in
turn appointed Tilly as keeper of the screws; Jessic
wielded the screwdriver, and Hettie stood by with the
hammer for the difficult bits that required a more
aggressive approach. A happy hour of laughter went
by, and eventually the bench was complete and ready
for the sunny days that would surely come after such
a cruel winter.

Tilly was beginning to feel exhausted. She had
made a remarkable recovery, but the day's excitement
had taken its toll and all she really wanted now was a
peaceful evening in front of the fire with Hettie. The
Butters' party looked like it would go on for some

time, and Betty had started to threaten Christmas tea and charades. Hettie noticed that Tilly had run out of steam and decided to make their excuses before they got caught up in the evening's entertainment. Collecting up their presents, they bade farewell to Bruiser, Jessie and the Butters, and crept back downstairs to the sanctuary of their own little room.

# CHAPTER THIRTY

The fire had burnt down low, and Hettie jabbed at it with the poker and added some kindling; it responded instantly, and within minutes the flames were dancing in the grate. 'Shall we try our new pyjamas?' Tilly suggested. 'They look lovely and warm, and we still have lots of presents to open.'

'I think we should leave most of them until tomorrow. Boxing Day is always a bit of a let-down, so we could have another Christmas Day instead. I've got one more present to give you now, though.'

Tilly beamed, pulled off her cardigan and wriggled into her new striped pyjamas. They were slightly on the big side, but she turned the sleeves up and Hettie had to admit that she did look very striking in them. 'I think we'll have to keep these for best – maybe on business trips and things like that,' she said, kicking off her day clothes, too, and replacing them with her new outfit.

Tilly was slightly disappointed, and said so. 'If we have to wait for business trips, we'll never get to wear them. They're too nice to live in the filing cabinet.'

Hettie was admiring herself in the mirror above the fireplace, and conceded that there was something quite decadent about wearing monogrammed pyjamas around the house; anyway, as Tilly had said, it was a rare thing indeed for the No. 2 Feline Detective Agency to be called away from home on an overnight case that required best pyjamas.

She braved the cold to fetch the two remaining presents from the shopping trolley by the bread ovens. The Butters' party was still in full swing, and the strains of Tijuana Brass – with vocal contributions from those still standing – crept down the stairs. 'We'll have to give Bruiser his alarm clock tomorrow,' she said as she came back into the room. 'Judging by the noise from upstairs, I doubt he's in a fit state to unwrap anything.'

'There are parcels for Jessie as well,' said Tilly. 'Maybe we could have a Boxing Day tea party tomorrow and hand them out then.'

'That's an excellent idea. But open this one now.'

Tilly took the parcel and sat on her cushion by the fire to open it. She patted and sniffed it, trying to guess, but gave up and ripped the paper off. She stared at the blanket and then at the plug on the end of it. 'Is it a magic carpet or something like that?'

Hettie laughed. 'Well, it *is* quite magic, I suppose. It's an electric blanket.' She lay the blanket out on Tilly's cushion and plugged it in, turning the control to 'hot'. 'Right – you sit on it and see what happens.'

Tilly did as she was told and purred as the warmth spread to the whole of her body. Seeing her contentment, Hettie joined her on the blanket and they sat together, enjoying the warmth and peace of their own Christmas.

Hettie suddenly remembered her new pipe and reached for it on the mantelpiece, dislodging the business letter which they'd left unopened. It floated down in front of the fire, and she looked at it a little more closely. 'This letter has an odd smell about it. If I didn't know better, I'd say it smelt of fish.'

In spite of the electric blanket, Tilly froze.

Hettie turned the letter over. 'And look at this! It's one of those old-fashioned seals. It looks like a crab has been stamped into it.'

Tilly put her paws up to her ears to block out Hettie's voice. 'Please don't open it!' she shouted. 'I can't bear it. It's happening all over again!'

Hettie was startled by Tilly's reaction, but she suddenly remembered some of the details of her nightmare. 'You really think that this letter has come from Crabstock Manor, don't you?' Tilly nodded.

Hettie shrugged her shoulders. 'Well, we're far too busy having a lovely Christmas to find out, aren't we?' She tossed the unopened letter into the fire, and the two friends watched it burn. 'Time to try out my new pipe, I think,' said Hettie, reaching for her catnip.

'Lovely,' said Tilly.

# ACKNOWLEDGEMENTS

Thank you to all at Allison & Busby for their continued support for this series.

When Nicola and I bought our cottage on the Cornish coast over fifteen years ago, it was to be a weekend retreat from the cares of a frantic city life. The reality was very different. We made ourselves at home, embracing the Cornish way of life, its people, and its magic. Even our cats, Hettie and Tilly, were never happier than when sitting on a window sill, staring out to sea.

This book was inspired by friends and characters in our village. Thank you to Russell Perkins for teaching me to steer a boat out to sea, and to Sandy for her friendship, love and support over the years. Their cat, Sooty, makes a very fine hero.

For me, no Cornish book is complete without a nod to Daphne du Maurier, who – like me – came as a stranger to this land and was captivated enough to plant roots in Cornwall's soil.